MW01716988

Perfectly UNEXPECTED

KAILY HART

Ellora's Cave
Romantica®
www.EllorasCave.com

Picture This

Desperate and young, Jillian Moore did something she knew would one day come back to bite her in the ass. She'd posed nude. For money. Years later, and on the fast track to a successful career, she's still haunted by her mistake. She can't help but wonder when her past will catch up with her.

Samuel Steele is not short on female attention, but the women who warm his bed pale in comparison to the fantasy he's created of the seductive temptress in the painting hanging prominently in his bedroom. A fantasy that has ruined his once-satisfying sex life. When he discovers that her exact likeness works in his building—works for *him*, in fact—things get interesting. Perhaps there's hope for his sex life after all...

Pay Up

Neighbor. Friend. *Lover.*

At least that's what Carly Wagner wanted Rio Reyes to be. She'd settled for two out of three for almost a year and it just wasn't enough. Not anymore. When Rio proposes a bet—of the sexual variety—she knows it's out of character and he's not really serious, yet she can't resist. The payoff could mean finally getting her hands on the gorgeous firefighter she's drooled over since she moved in next door.

The timing had never seemed right for him and Carly, but that hadn't stopped Rio from imagining wild and wicked things about her. It had been a joke—*sort of*—but Rio's shocked when she takes him up on the dumbass bet. Now he's in a world of hurt, because regardless of who wins, he might be crossing a line he never thought he would, and jeopardizing a friendship that means more to him than anything.

PLAY ME

Lily Hamilton had her quiet, predictable life all mapped out, including a hot-shot attorney for a fiancé. That is until she catches him screwing around and takes off in his prized Mercedes, for once not giving a damn where she's headed. How clichéd is *that*?

Gabriel Jackson is raw and disillusioned. Driving a tow truck is a far cry from the dangerous career he turned his back on, but when he finds the classy blonde in a dangerous part of LA, he's immediately back in the role of protector.

Lily is hot and sweet and so out of his league it's not funny, yet Gabe can't deny the sizzling heat between them. He thinks he wants hard, fast and rough—until he gets his hands on her. He knows he should stay the hell away, but Lily makes him feel, *really* feel, for the first time in two years. Is she just slumming or can she see beyond the harsh, broken façade to the man beneath? A man who dreams of making her his?

An Ellora's Cave Publication

www.ellorascave.com

Perfectly Unexpected

ISBN 9781419965029

Edited by Grace Bradley.
Designer and Photographer: Syneca.
Model: Kory.

Trade paperback publication 2011

PERFECTLY UNEXPECTED

Kaily Hart

PICTURE THIS

Dedication

I'd like to dedicate my debut book to all the aspiring authors out there. Every. Single. One of you. Don't give up, just don't, because all of you deserve to have people read the stories of your heart.

I'd also like to thank Rula Sinara. Whether you know it or not, you've been my rock. I guess it was fate, my friend.

To Cari Quinn. You're an awesome writer and have been so generous and supportive. I appreciate everything you've done.

And to D. See? I told you so.

Chapter One

Christ, he was a sick fuck.

Sam rubbed his hand over the rough stubble on his jaw, the raspy sound loud in the quiet room. Carla, Carrie, or whatever the hell her name was, had left. Hell, she hadn't been able to get away fast enough once she'd figured it out. He could still smell the unmistakable scent of sex. It was thick and heavy in the air and wafted up from the ruined sheets he was lying on every time he moved. It'd been good—hard, fast and impersonal, just how he liked it. Okay, so it'd gone to crap at the end, but he'd gotten his rocks off and had no complaints in that regard. She'd been gorgeous and built, with a tongue that was more talented than most and a way of moving her hips when she rode him that had almost blown the top of his head off. So what was his problem and what the *fuck* was he doing? He shouldn't still want to, shouldn't need to—

He shook his head in equal parts resignation and disgust as his hand unerringly found his hard cock. God, here he was. Playing with himself like some horny teenager, fantasizing about pussy and wild, rough, out of control sex—as if he didn't get enough as it was. It shouldn't even be possible for him to be this hard again this fast. He shuddered at the sensation as he wrapped his fingers around his shaft and parted his legs to give himself more room. He couldn't prevent the groan of anticipation when he reached down and cupped his balls with his other hand.

Eyes riveted to the opposite wall, he gave in to the raging need that had plagued him for weeks, a need that was unrelenting in its fierce grip. A need he knew he couldn't fight for long. It just made it worse.

Yeah, he'd become one sick fuck all right.

* * * * *

"Well, thank you for your time and for the information. It was very helpful."

Not.

Jillian put the phone down a little harder than she'd intended. It slammed back into the cradle with a sharp crack that more than matched her mood.

Dammit.

It'd been sold, *again,* three months earlier. Private auction, anonymous bidder and there was no way for her to find out who'd bought it. All she knew for sure was that it'd been a man. It figured. *Damn,* she'd been close this time. Not that she would have been able to afford to make even one bid herself. It had opened at fifteen thousand and after some fast and furious bidding had finally gone for a cool seventy-five thousand—*dollars.* Jeez, she'd probably be paying off her student loans for another twenty years and some guy had dropped seventy-five grand on a *picture*?

Jillian sighed. She wasn't even sure what she'd do if she could uncover the identity of the new owner. She'd kept telling herself she'd be able to buy it one day once she got established. She'd planned on it, she'd *counted* on it. It was why she'd tried her damndest to keep track of it for the past ten years. Her only hope now was that it would sit in some private collection, gathering dust and never see the light of day. Yeah, right. She'd never, ever been that lucky. All those years ago, who would have thought? Deep down though she'd known and it had plagued her ever since. When she least expected it, it was going to come back and bite her on the ass. She just knew it.

* * * * *

"Sam? Man, are you even listening to me?"

Sam couldn't tear his eyes off her. The dark luster of her hair, the curve of her cheek, something about the shape of her body. It just now occurred to him, but he'd seen her around the building before. He'd noticed her legs he remembered, appreciated the toned lengths, the shapely calves and too easily imagined how they'd look wrapped around his waist or up around her ears. And her mouth. God, the things he'd thought about her mouth.

How could I have forgotten that?

As soon as the thought formed he knew the answer. He had a strict hands-off rule at work that he'd never broken, not even in his head. Until her. He'd *made* himself forget.

He watched her mouth curve into a smile and his dick twitched in immediate response. Something flared low and sharp in his gut. It was a sensation he didn't think he'd ever felt before, at least without some form of specific and intentional stimulation.

"Who's that?" he demanded.

"Who?"

He heard rather than saw Duncan's puzzlement. He motioned across the expanse of the elegant lobby. "The woman there. Slim, dark hair, black suit. Talking to the blonde."

"I thought you didn't fuck around with the staff?"

Sam's balls tightened in a rush. The explicit image he got was shocking. Not just because it was of *her*—on her knees in front of him while he fucked her from behind—but because he hadn't been able to censor it, or control his body's reaction to it. Sam shot him a glare. He was in no mood to be trifled with.

Duncan cleared his throat. "Ah, sorry, I think her name's Jennifer, something like that. She works in Finance. Or maybe it's Legal."

"Jillian?" he managed to choke out. "Could her name be Jillian?"

"I...maybe. Why?"

"Last time I checked you were head of Human Resources, Duncan."

"Jesus, Sam, we have over four thousand employees, two thousand in this building alone. I can't personally keep track of all of them. I haven't worked with her directly. She's probably—"

"Find out. I want her file on my desk in ten minutes."

"What's got into you?"

Sam took a deep breath. "Schedule a meeting with her."

"A meeting?"

"Yeah, with me."

"You don't know where she works or what she does in your company, but you want a meeting with her? *Why*?"

Sam felt the impatience he'd tried to contain roar through him. He wasn't used to having his orders questioned and he sure as hell wasn't used to explaining himself to anyone.

"Because I'm the fucking boss and I said so."

* * * * *

So, she'd dropped everything as ordered and hightailed it up here. *Now what*?

She hadn't had time to grab even a quick bite for lunch and her stomach was beginning to churn in protest. Of course, it wasn't everyday someone at her level got a personal summons to the big boss's office, so that might have something to do with it.

So, what the hell did he want with *her*? She hadn't done anything. Had she? And if she had, wouldn't he want to talk to her manager? Okay, so the analysis she'd done on the Bourke deal hadn't exactly been her best work, but it was still better than anything anyone else here could have done. As usual, she hadn't gotten any credit for it. Her manager was a pain in the neck, a frustrating pain in the neck because she'd gotten into the predicament of allowing him to take credit for her work.

Well, not exactly take credit, but anything he presented up the chain was never individually recognized. Had it come back to bite him on the ass and he'd thrown her under the bus? Even if the IT geeks had somehow tracked her checking out the naked firefighter calendar last week, it would come down through the department head. *Wouldn't it*?

Jillian took a deep breath. "Am I in some kind of trouble?"

She'd always liked the direct approach and she wasn't sure how long she could stand the suspense, particularly on an empty stomach. If she needed to go clear out her desk, she'd prefer to know sooner, rather than later. And if she didn't? Well then, she had about fifty unread emails, a voicemail light that wouldn't quit blinking, a spreadsheet still to get through and a meeting due to start in—*crap*—fifteen minutes ago.

"Depends on what you consider...trouble."

Jillian blinked. His response was delivered in a slow, sexy drawl. If she hadn't already been nervous from the intense scrutiny he'd given her since she'd walked into his fancy office that would have amped things up considerably.

"Ms. Moore, Jillian, why don't you sit down?"

Oh my God, Samuel Steele was a walking, talking wet dream.

She'd drooled from afar plenty, but up close he was downright gorgeous. Every woman in the place, and even some of the guys, had checked out his tight butt, flat abs and broad shoulders, and although he'd never worn anything but a suit to the office, that didn't stop imaginations from running riot. His hair was dark and thick, his skin tanned, and regardless of the time of day, his jaw always seemed darkened with at least a day's beard growth. And his eyes. She'd never been close enough to make out their color before, but they were a dark, piercing gray. They should have looked cold, but the way he was looking at her made her wonder if someone had turned off the air-conditioning.

She swallowed at the sudden lump in her throat. "Mr. Steele."

"Sam. Call me Sam."

"Ah, Sam, what—"

"Sit down. Please."

Jillian's stomach jolted. She knew he had to be busier than her, so if it was going to take some time and she needed to be sitting, well, it could only be bad, really bad. She clasped her hands together in her lap as she relented and sat in front of his heavy desk. He lowered his long length onto its edge in front of her, totally filling her visual field and putting his crotch directly in her line of sight. With his suit pants bunched around his muscular thighs, the fabric hugged and accentuated the bulge between his legs. What could she say? It looked impressive to say the least.

Oh God.

The roiling of her stomach and the slight tremors she could feel along the length of her legs weren't just because of a feeling of dread. Truthfully? In the dead of the night when her body burned, when it craved a man's touch and she brought herself relief? *His* was the face she pictured above her, *his* were the hands she visualized on her holding her down, *his* was the body she imagined pleasuring her. *Crap.* Now she'd been close enough to actually smell him. It was something expensive, but rugged, and she wasn't getting it out of her head anytime soon.

She cleared her throat, but her voice still sounded scratchy. "Mr.…Sam, what do you—"

"Have dinner with me."

Jillian thought she might have gasped. Okay, she was pretty sure she did.

He wanted to date her? He'd specifically demanded her presence in his office, insisting she drop everything she was doing, because he wanted to ask her out on a *date?*

She'd never heard any hint of him coming on to any of the women at Steele Enterprises. Quite the opposite in fact. It was common knowledge throughout the company that he didn't involve himself with any woman who worked for him. It caused a lot of disappointment among the female ranks on a regular basis.

His eyes were locked on hers, probably to gauge her reaction. No one had ever looked at her quite like that before, as if they wanted to...devour her. It was explicit, as if he'd stripped every stitch of clothing off her in his mind and was memorizing her curves. It should have shocked and offended her; it should have disgusted her on some level at least. He was the owner and CEO of the company after all, her boss, but the punch to her stomach told her what she felt was something entirely different.

Keep it together, Jillian.

She lifted her chin to be sure she met his gaze dead-on. "I've heard you don't date anyone who works for you. That it's always been a hard and fast rule."

He rubbed at the back of his neck. "Yeah."

Jillian worked hard to keep her body toned and fit. She knew she was attractive and tried to make the best of her looks, but no way was she the drop-dead gorgeous type. Guys didn't fall all over themselves to meet her, they didn't beg for her phone number, they didn't look back at her if she passed them on the street and she knew she didn't make that much of a lasting impression. At least her last boyfriend hadn't thought so. Besides, she'd heard Sam Steele had a penchant for models—of the leggy, blonde variety.

"So, why me?"

After a slight hesitation, he glanced down at himself. It was a somewhat rueful look. When Jillian followed his gaze, she felt the flush she couldn't prevent flood her face. There was no way he could hide it the way he was sitting. It wasn't the cut of his pants that caused the tenting and it was obvious he'd lucked out in the size department. Big-time.

When he clearly wasn't going to say anything, Jillian tried to remind herself a sophisticated woman would not be fighting the urge to put her hands to her heated cheeks or over her eyes.

"This is clichéd I know, but I've heard you change women as often as you change your underwear."

"So?"

She almost sputtered. *Almost*. She'd expected him to try and skirt around it at least. "So, I don't go for one-time, one-night casual sex."

His jaw clenched. "Once isn't going to cut it, Jillian."

She felt the heat sear through her. It wasn't a slow wash. It was an immediate flush over her entire body ending in a heated burn between her legs and a sharp tug low in her abdomen. Perhaps it was the intensity in his eyes or it might have been the way her name sounded rumbling from his chest. Or maybe it was just the fact that he'd told her he wanted to have sex with her in no uncertain terms. She squirmed a little on the chair, barely preventing a sharp intake of breath as the seam of her pants pulled tight across her sensitive flesh, rubbing directly against her clitoris. She was wet and hot and aching.

"You want to go out on a…date? For a night?"

"Not particularly, but I will if you require it."

Jillian frowned. "Require it?"

"Yeah. Before you'll let me fuck you."

Jillian's heart slammed against her chest. Hard. She wet her suddenly dry lips, tried to think of something to say—*anything*—but her mind was a complete blank. Well, except for the image of them twined together, on his desk, mostly naked, her pants around her ankles and her—

Jillian jumped when someone suddenly knocked and walked into the office unannounced. She released the breath she hadn't been aware she'd been holding as Sam looked away from her, his expression fierce at the interruption.

"Sam, could you—"

"Get the fuck out," he snarled. "The next person who comes in here is fired. *Understood*?"

Jillian heard a quiet murmur and then the door closed quietly but quickly, leaving them in the cocooned silence once more.

"Have you lost your mind?" Jillian demanded.

"Possibly."

"They'll think... *God*, I'm not sure what they'll think. You're the boss. You'll be excused anything because you call the shots. *Me*? I'll be the brunt of gossip and innuendo for months."

"Jillian. I can tell you're the direct, up-front type. You want the truth?"

Did she? She took a deep breath. She wasn't so sure, but she nodded anyway.

"I want you in my bed. Tonight."

Everything went still inside her. How long had it been since she'd had sex—actually had sex—with a man, not a battery-operated device? She could barely remember, which should have told her something. It had never been like this though. It had always been after she'd gotten to know someone, usually after a few dates, a gradual buildup until she felt she was ready to give herself, to share something of herself. She'd never, ever had a one-night stand. She wasn't actually considering it, was she?

"Th-this could be construed as sexual harassment, you know," she managed shakily.

"You feel it too, don't you?"

"*It*?"

He leaned forward, his face only inches from hers. This close she could see that his eyes were actually rimmed by a darker gray around the edges. They were intense and...really quite beautiful. She saw his nostrils flare briefly. "I can smell how aroused you are," he whispered.

"You cannot!"

He laughed. It was quick, but she got a flash of very white, even teeth. "Okay, I can't. But I want to." He ran his gaze down her length in a look she almost felt. "You have my imagination working overtime."

That made two of them. Jillian had never felt *this* before, whatever it was. He turned her on like no guy ever had and she was usually the slow burn type, but her body seemed to have a mind of its own. Her bed had been empty since she'd come to work here, even some time before that. Cold, lonely, unsatisfying and *empty*. Could she really do it? Be calculating about it? No emotions to get in the way, no feelings to be hurt, nothing but pleasure, because if she was sure of anything, she was sure he'd give her pleasure. She'd been guilty of listening to the rumor mill where he was concerned and if there was any truth to them, he'd more than live up to the explicit promises in his gaze. Not to mention the bulge in his pants. A night of sex, pure and simple. Did she dare?

She had to know first though. Perhaps it was why she'd never heard any hint of him messing around with anyone at the office.

"Will it… Will this help my career in any way?"

Chapter Two

Sam thought about lying. He did. It wouldn't be the first time a chick had expected something in return, in appreciation, for granting him the use of her body. He no longer gave gifts or favors for sex, *ever,* but he'd never had such a violent and intense reaction to a woman before either.

Lust he knew. Lust he recognized and acted on when it suited him and when it worked itself out of his system? He moved on. This was something else entirely or maybe it was just stronger than anything he'd felt before. Yeah, that must be it. That he was acting completely out of character registered on some vague level, but… *Fuck,* up close the resemblance was uncanny. And her name was Jillian. It couldn't be a coincidence, could it? It wasn't just that there were similarities, she looked exactly the same. Jillian was clearly older, but it was the same dark hair, the same clear, honey skin and the eyes… They weren't exactly inviting him to do whatever he wanted to her, but they were the same shade of intense blue. Her body—just thinking about the body she might be hiding under the conservative pantsuit and what she might look like between her legs—kept him painfully hard. Somewhat embarrassing considering his erection was practically staring her in the face.

He hadn't been this out of control of his body since…well, since last night when he'd jacked off in front of the damn painting again. A painting that hung prominently at the foot of his bed, a painting he'd literally been obsessed with since he'd first seen it, a painting that looked remarkably like his senior financial analyst, Jillian Moore.

He wanted her with a desperation that had him holding himself back with an effort from jumping her, but he couldn't lie. He couldn't, not even to ensure he got in her pants.

"No," he ground out, knowing he may have just blown his chances if she thought that's the way he operated. Or if it was the way she did. Thinking she might be open to using sex to progress herself didn't sit well with him. *At all.*

"Fucking me will not improve your chances of promotion or your pay. Neither will it be detrimental to your career. This has nothing to do with work. This is just you and me, getting naked and getting off together. You've worked here for eighteen months, Jillian. I may be tough, demanding and moody as hell, but you have to know I'm fair."

He took a deep breath. It would kill him, but she'd have to take it or leave it. He was already thinking on his next tactic when he saw her nod. Jesus, it was so slight he might have missed it, could have misinterpreted it, maybe it didn't mean what he thought.

"Okay, then." She sighed. "If you'd said yes, I would have had to tell you to go screw yourself."

Sam tried to hide the tremendous relief he felt and the sense of triumph, not to mention the images that slammed into him when he thought about who and what he'd rather "screw". It wouldn't do to gloat. It wasn't exactly an agreement, but he'd run with it anyway.

"We'll leave here after work. Six. Okay?"

Sam couldn't remember the last time he'd left the office at six, maybe never, but waiting until the end of the day was going to be torture as it was. He'd be damned if he'd wait any longer than he needed to. He knew he was pushing it, but if he knew anything at all, it was women, and he had her—right where he wanted her.

"Ah... I have my car here and I need to do a few things first. Could I meet you somewhere?"

He didn't like it, but he'd pushed enough. He sighed. He was damn tired of resorting to fucking women because of their resemblance to his first foray into fine art. And if that wasn't bad enough? Last night, with an experienced, beautiful woman in his bed, moaning and bucking under him, he'd realized with shock that he needed the stimulation of it to actually get off. And that was just fucking unacceptable. He just wanted to get this *thing,* whatever it was, out of his system and get on with his life.

He tempered the surge of anticipation and refused to let himself consider the possibility she wouldn't show. He'd offered, but dinner was the last thing he wanted. He wanted *her* with a force he couldn't quantify and the thought of having to go through a "getting to know you" meal just so he could get her naked, had him almost growling with frustration. Man, who was he kidding? He just wanted to fuck her brains out all night long, pure and simple. He suddenly wanted her in his space, on his ground. He hoped like hell he knew what he was doing. He'd always sworn he'd never sleep with anyone who worked for him. With everything else he'd had to worry about, building the company with his blood and sweat from nothing, he'd never wanted the potential liability. Yet, here he was, ready to throw all that out the window. For *her*.

Jillian's heart was beating so fast she thought it might leap from her chest. Had she just agreed to have wild, no-strings sex? A one-night stand with her *boss*? *Tonight*? To say she'd let personal grooming slide some recently was probably an understatement. Waxing the bikini area, shaving your legs every single day, getting a pedicure, didn't seem so critical when you and your vibrator were the only ones who got to see it.

Sam unfolded his big body, stepped around to his desk and roughly scribbled something on a sheet of paper he all but shoved at her.

"My place. Six thirty."

Arrogant prick. She almost told him to go to hell right then, but why should it matter? She knew what this was and her eyes were wide open. And *God,* the heat and dampness between her legs was becoming uncomfortable.

Jillian glanced down at the dark, bold scrawl. His address. It was a nice neighborhood, more than nice, but it didn't give her much time. She shook her head, already figuring out everything she needed to do before she got there. "Eight," she countered, seriously wondering whether she'd chicken out or not.

He hesitated a heartbeat before giving her a curt nod. He wasn't happy.

Well, tough.

She'd never done anything like this before. *Never.* Was there an etiquette involved in these things? She wasn't sure what would happen or how this would play out exactly, but the nervous anticipation in the meantime just might kill her. "Wh-what should I wear?"

His gaze centered on her. Hot, direct, carnal. "Doesn't matter. You won't have it on very long."

Okay, that probably gave her a pretty good idea.

* * * * *

Jillian took a deep, steadying breath. It didn't help much. Actually, it didn't help at all. Sam's gaze was riveted on her with the same look she'd last seen from him and a few hours hadn't lessened its impact.

"Take off your panties."

Jillian swallowed. It was a demand, there was no question about it, but his voice was rough and husky.

What the hell had she gotten herself into?

She'd chosen a short, denim dress that hugged her curves, buttoned down the front and flared in a slight a-line she thought was flattering. She'd left the top two buttons open to give a hint of cleavage and the bottom two undone which provided glimpses of her now smooth thighs when she moved. That left only three buttons that held the entire dress on her. She'd thought it looked sexy, young and accessible, but perhaps she should have gone for something more alluring, more sophisticated? What she wouldn't give to see his reaction if she could have said she wasn't wearing any panties.

"Hello to you, too," she managed.

"Sorry," Sam added when she didn't move from her stance by his front door. "I'm not up for any preliminaries. I want you so badly I'm seriously about to split the seams on these pants."

He was still dressed as he'd been at the office, but he'd removed his jacket and tie and rolled up his sleeves. He didn't sound the least apologetic, but at his comment, Jillian couldn't help but center her gaze between his legs. She could see the ridge that could only come from a massive erection.

Oh God.

Hoping like hell he didn't notice the tremors in her hands, Jillian reached up under her dress and tugged off her panties. She cringed. She knew the move probably looked awkward, not to mention downright demure. Before she could decide what she was going to do with them, Sam stepped forward and grabbed them from her. She watched, mesmerized as he raised the black satin thong up to his nose and inhaled deeply. His jaw clenched, his lids flickered and Jillian shook at the look in his eyes.

"*Fuck.* You smell incredible."

He flung them aside and grasped her hand. Without taking his eyes from hers, he walked backward, pulling her with him farther into the house until he sat down in a large arm chair.

Her heart thundered so strongly it was almost deafening. She tried to calm herself by taking a few slow breaths, but her stomach felt like it did on the plunges of a roller coaster, only it never ended, and it was impossible to catch her breath.

Bracketing her hips with his hands, he stretched his long legs out in front of him between hers and eased her forward slowly.

"As soon as I saw you in this dress, I knew what I was going to do."

Jillian trembled as he began to undo the buttons, one slow tug at a time. She hadn't worn a bra, she hadn't needed to, and soon she stood bared before him, the dress hanging open from her shoulders.

"Christ, look at you."

Jillian sighed at the look in his eyes and the reverence in his voice. She'd never seen that look from another guy before, she was sure of it. It was completely focused on her, watching her every move and more than liking what he saw. His gaze wandered over her full aching breasts, across her abdomen and centered between her legs. It gave her an incredible sense of empowerment. He wanted her. Really wanted *her*, and he made no attempt to hide it. All of her unease vanished in an instant.

He skimmed the folds between her legs with the back of his hand and she felt heat and moisture bloom for him. "You're completely bare, silky, so soft and smooth. *Beautiful*," he breathed.

She kept her eyes open and trained on his with difficulty. She hadn't had the time to get a wax. She'd shaved though, as close as she could. She'd tried to leave a tantalizing line of hair, but had screwed it up and ended up taking it all off. Now she was fiercely glad.

"I need to taste. Come here."

Oh God, oh God.

Jillian jumped at the sensation of his hot breath against the skin of her abdomen as his hands urged her forward and he leaned in. He licked her in a slow, long swipe along the crease of her leg where it met her body, as if she was some tasty treat he was savoring.

She quivered when he groaned. She gasped when his tongue traced up the middle of her torso, dipping into her bellybutton and up between her breasts, his hands gently pushing the dress down her arms. The fact that it didn't fall at her feet made her realize she had the fingers of both hands buried in his thick, dark hair, holding him to her, urging him on.

He licked first one nipple, teasing, taunting licks, then the other, alternating between them until she couldn't help the involuntary movements of her lower body against his thighs where she straddled him. He wasn't sucking hard, pulling or biting at them. He didn't use his hands, only his mouth, and he was lapping at her, mindless flicks and licks and the action sent a shaft of pure sensation straight to her clit. It felt as if the smallest touch from him there and she'd be done.

"I can feel how hot and wet you are through my pants," he rasped.

"Oh God, Sam..." So could she. She wasn't sure she'd ever been this wet before. She could feel the slight trickle from her body that came as if in sync with each lick of his insistent tongue on her nipples.

"Put your knees up on the arms of the chair."

He wanted her to do...*what*?

He urged her up with firm hands on her hips until she knelt on each of the sturdy arms. She clutched the back of the chair to steady herself, gasping when he splayed a large, broad palm across her abdomen.

Was he trembling? She thought she felt it in the hands holding her, but it seemed unlikely for a guy like him. He had a different woman in his bed each week, didn't he?

She jumped when he rubbed a thumb back and forth across her soaked clit and tried to just concentrate on breathing, and not falling from her precarious perch. She throbbed, ached, burned and then she couldn't think of anything as he slowly inserted a thick finger inside her.

"Pretty," he groaned. "So fucking pretty."

"Sam," she moaned and flexed involuntarily around him. Just his finger felt large inside her and oh so good. He was watching her, watching his hand, his finger, as he moved it slowly in and out of her, retreating all the way and then sinking back up as far as he could go. She was vaguely aware of him sliding down in the chair and then his mouth was against her too.

Her whole body jerked at the contact. The whimpers she heard must have come from her, but all her focus, her attention, was centered between her legs and the sensations he aroused in her. In that instant she knew she'd let this man do whatever he wanted to do with her body and the realization scared the hell out of her.

Fighting for breath, struggling for some semblance of sanity, Jillian looked down. He was licking and sucking on her but his eyes, dark and raw, watched her, causing a heat she'd never experienced before to burn through her. She couldn't tear her gaze away. Helpless in her need, she couldn't have prevented the involuntary movements of her hips, even if she wanted to.

"That's it. Fuck my mouth, baby," he growled.

Shocked, Jillian realized she was grinding herself against him, pushing herself hard against his mouth, his tongue. Soon he wasn't moving his head at all. It was all her as she moved herself back and forth against him, back and forth, controlling the pressure where she wanted it, needed it, her movements frenzied until she… Oh God…

He grasped her hips and lifted her up, freeing his mouth. Cool air washed against flesh that was hot, wet and aching. Jillian cried out, she couldn't help it. She'd been so close. She had to bite her lip to stop herself from begging him to continue, offering him anything if he'd just do it again.

"Not yet," he ground out, his hot breath sawing in and out against her thighs. "I want to be inside you, my body inside yours the first time you come for me."

Jillian gasped when he cupped her ass in his big hands and stood. It was a single, fluid action and showcased a strength he kept well hidden beneath the conservative suits. She tightened her arms around his neck, her legs somehow ending up wrapped around his lean waist. His body was hot and hard and pressed as she was against him, she could feel the thunder of his heartbeat mirroring her own. As he moved purposefully through the house she tried to concentrate on easing her breathing, but all she could think about was that soon he'd be taking care of the empty, stinging ache between her legs with something a lot bigger than his finger.

She'd expected to be dropped roughly onto the big bed. Instead Sam eased her down almost gently. She shivered a little at the coolness of the sheets against her hot skin. He'd carried her. She wasn't exactly small, but he'd actually picked her up and carried her. She glanced quickly around the big room. She didn't know what she was expecting, but it looked just like any other bedroom. No circular bed or mirrored ceiling anywhere in sight.

"This is a guest room. I don't… I've never had a woman in here."

Was she that transparent? And why would he care enough to mention it?

Sam jerked at the buttons of his shirt, drawing her attention to the tiny square packet already clasped in his hand. Thankfully he'd thought of protection because until now? She hadn't. Throat dry, eyes wide, her body still throbbing between her legs from his touch, Jillian watched as he jerked at and removed every piece of his clothing. By the time he kicked his dark briefs to the side and went about sheathing himself, it was all she could do not to squirm on the bed.

"Hurry," she whispered raggedly before she could stop herself. Could you instantaneously combust from being turned-on?

He looked like a male model—all rippling golden skin over ripped, hard muscles—except there was a harshness, a roughness about him that proclaimed him all man. A man obviously very much in his prime. He definitely didn't spend all of his time behind a desk.

She knew his shape, but not even her overactive imagination could have prepared her for the impact of him naked. His chest was covered by a sprinkling of dark hair that narrowed in a line down his torso and into the thick thatch at his groin. Holy hell, he was big. Long and thick and hard. It figured. Rich, successful, hot and hung. He had it all going on. No wonder he had no shortage of women willing to warm his bed or wherever else took his fancy.

Jillian's mouth went dry when he stepped to the bed and lowered himself over her, using his heavy hair-roughened thighs to spread her own and centered himself above her. Just like he'd said, he really wasn't up for preliminaries. Bracing himself on one arm, he grasped his cock and rubbed himself back and forth through her slick folds slowly, applying just enough pressure to have her gasping and arching up into him. She grasped his thick shoulders. The condom felt a little cool against her hot, pulsating flesh. Just for an instant, it brought home exactly what it was she was doing. She was having sex with her boss, here in his house, a man essentially a stranger to her—but it felt like nothing she'd ever experienced before.

He grunted softly as he began to slowly push himself into her.

Jillian moved her hips to adjust to his angle. He was so big, his powerful body holding hers down against the mattress, dominating her completely. She placed one hand low against his abdomen, just above his coarse hair line as he began to move.

"Sam," she implored, not really sure what she was asking or expecting, not wanting him to stop, but needing to—

"It's okay," he managed through clenched teeth. "I've got it."

He pushed in and out again and she moaned, both her hands finding their way to the smooth skin of his lean hips, as if her hold could somehow control the depth of his thrusts into her. Her fingers clutched him harder as he moved back and then forward again. She could feel the bones of his hips, but he was covered in hard, thick, lean muscle.

His thrusts into her were slow and shallow—patient—allowing her body the time to get accustomed to his. She whimpered at the sensation of stretching and the friction against her swollen clit, her moisture slowly easing his path, as he gradually increased the depth of his penetration. It had been so long since she'd felt a man inside her. She'd almost forgotten the sensation of heat and fullness, although it had never felt quite like this. All at once she wanted more, she wanted all of him.

"Sam, please, *please*—"

"It's okay. I've got you sweetheart."

Chapter Three

Sam tried to concentrate on his breathing, anything but the tightness wrapped around his cock like a clenched fist. *Sweetheart*? Where the hell had that come from? Sure, he'd been guilty of dropping an endearment when a name slipped his mind. "Baby" was usually more like it though. He had no trouble remembering Jillian's name, so...*sweetheart*? Jeez, he was really losing it.

He was balanced on the knife edge of a control he'd always prided himself on. Man, he knew he was moving fast, even for him, but he couldn't bear it if she changed her mind. Even if she hadn't told him, he would have known she didn't do this kind of thing that often. The snugness of her body told him that much—*and* that she probably hadn't had sex in a long time. It pleased the hell out of him.

He was also fiercely glad he'd never gotten around to christening the spare room. He'd slept in it himself a time or two when he'd had a woman stay over and hadn't been able to sleep, but the room had no residual memories of another woman. It would just be her.

All at once he thrust to the hilt and couldn't hold back the deep groan that rumbled from him. She was so hot, so tight, so fucking slick. It felt incredible, she felt incredible. He felt the tingle in his balls, the shudder that shot down his spine and settled low in his back. He was already close, really fucking close. It was going to take an effort not to come too soon. In this at least he was a gentleman. Ladies first. *Always*.

Sam gritted his teeth, looked down and got a punch to his gut at the sight of her sprawled beneath him. Leveraged as he was up on straight arms, the view was magnificent. Her dark hair was mussed and spread out on the bed around her head. Her eyes were half closed, almost as if she could barely keep them open and her cheeks were softly flushed. She was breathing in shallow pants, the breath forced from her body through her open mouth each time he pumped his cock deep into her.

Sam trailed his gaze down her body, past her gorgeous full breasts, which jiggled with each thrust, down across the slight curve of her stomach to between her legs. He lifted himself a fraction so he had a better view and gulped air into his oxygen-starved lungs. He couldn't tear his eyes away from the sight of them joined—her pussy tight around him, clasping and sucking him as he moved in and out in a rhythm he struggled to keep steady, when all he wanted to do was let go of the tight rein he had on his control and fuck her senseless.

He was vaguely aware of Jillian reaching up to him. Her fingers dug into the hair at the nape of his neck and she tugged once, twice. Without changing the depth or tempo of his thrusts, he fastened his gaze to hers in silent query. He wasn't hurting her, was he?

"Come down on me," she gasped, "I want to feel you against me."

Sam hesitated. This is why he rarely fucked face to face. It was too personal. He couldn't resist her plea though and lowered his big body down over hers, bracing himself above her on his forearms. The position meant his face was directly above hers, their eyes level. He saw her lids flicker and felt the clench of her fingers on his shoulders as he managed to go a little deeper with his next movement. They both groaned in unison.

Sam thought she'd wrap her legs around his hips, or better yet, his waist, but she twined her legs around him, her calves resting over his, anchoring him to her, into her deeply. It didn't give him a lot of room to maneuver, but *fuck* it felt good, too good for the conservative position—one he didn't usually care for all that much.

She moved against him in perfect counterpart. This close he could see every nuance of her expression as he moved in and out of her in a rhythm that soon had him struggling to draw in enough air and gritting his teeth again to ensure he didn't come. It was like nothing he'd ever felt before and all at once he wanted it to last.

And then he was kissing her, his mouth hard and rough against hers, his tongue sweeping into her mouth boldly and curling around her own. He mimicked the same rhythm of his cock inside her. He'd been so eager to get her into his bed he hadn't even taken the time to kiss her, to learn her flavor, to make even a token attempt at seducing her. No, the need riding him had been too strong, too urgent. He licked at her lips as he drew in a deep breath and swallowed her sharp sob.

He felt the prick of her nails at his shoulders. Normally he hated the sensation, but looking down into her face he'd bet his life it wasn't deliberate, and he kind of liked knowing she was so far gone she wasn't aware of what she was doing. Her eyes were closed and her head tipped back in utter abandon.

He flexed and she tightened anew around him. *Fuck.* He gasped at the sensation and hoped like hell she was with him because all at once he couldn't hold back any longer. It was his last coherent thought before his body was pistoning in and out of her uncontrollably, much more roughly than he intended, and he was lost as his release tore through him in deep pulses that reverberated throughout his entire body.

Sam dragged air into his lungs in harsh pulls as he came back to himself and to Jillian's hoarse voice filling his head.

"*Sam,* don't stop. Please, I'm—"

She arched under him, whimpering, her body taut and he felt the tremors rack her body. It suddenly dawned on him. He'd been concentrating on breathing deeply to calm his rapidly thudding heart, taking stock of the intense pleasure he'd just experienced and wondering what the fuck had happened to his renowned finesse, and she…

He pulled out of her awkwardly, rolled to his side and shakily pushed two fingers into her, thrusting deeply, trying his best to recreate the pace of his body in hers just moments earlier and using the heel of his palm to apply pressure to her clit.

She groaned, her head thrown back as she catapulted into a long, intense orgasm. *Fuck.* Watching her writhe like that in total abandon, her gorgeous body shuddering with the fierceness of her pleasure was the hottest thing he'd ever seen. He leaned down and licked her nipple, applying the flat of his tongue to her in the same rhythm as his hand. He smiled savagely when she gasped and jerked in response, her body spilling more of her wetness onto his hand and just like that she was on the brink of release. *Again.*

The pleasure. God, the pleasure. It had almost been more than she could bear and had bordered on pain, it had been so intense. She'd known, as soon as he'd moved inside her, the relentless entry and retreat of his big body in hers would push her toward an orgasm that was unlike anything she'd ever experienced before. Even now, struggling to draw in enough air, her body still throbbed with the aftermath of it. How long had passed? Minutes? Seconds? It could have been hours for all she knew. She'd been totally lost to everything.

Jillian cleared her throat with effort. "I'm sorry. I…"

"Sorry? No. Jesus, don't be sorry." Sam was lying next to her, his big hand still buried between her legs, his fingers rubbing gently over flesh still slick and swollen. "I'm not sure I've ever given a woman a multiple orgasm before. Actually, I figured it was pretty much a myth."

"Yeah, me too," she managed.

"That's never happened to you before?"

Jillian could do nothing but shake her head. Was he kidding? She'd overheard her last boyfriend tell his friend that fucking her was like "sticking his dick into a plank of wood".

Yeah, he'd been a gem all right. She'd had no idea her body was even capable of release like that. Even bringing herself to pleasure, knowing just how she liked it, being able to control every aspect of her orgasm, felt nothing like it'd just been with Sam. It was as if he had some direct line into her sexual psyche somehow and that was more than a little terrifying.

Just looking at him, knowing they'd had sex, that his body had been over her, in her, had the now familiar frisson of awareness simmering through her again. The strands of his thick hair were damp around his face and the muscles in his arms and shoulders gleamed with sweat. His breathing was still rough, his eyes dark and raw and intimate with the explicit knowledge he now had of her.

He slowly trailed his hand from between her legs. Jillian felt the wetness against the heat of her skin at the top of her thigh and swallowed against the dryness of her throat when he lifted his hand to his face and licked his palm in a long, slow swipe.

"Your cum tastes so fucking sweet," he groaned, sucking two of his fingers into his mouth. "Next time I won't be so quick off the mark. I want to ride that with you."

She probably hadn't been aware of it, but she'd panted his name as she came. Over and over in a chant that was probably forever etched in his brain. How fucking hot was that? Of all the women he'd been with, not a one had used his name like that. Almost like a litany, in total and utter abandon, breathy and raw.

She still had her shoes on. Actually, she was technically still wearing the dress. He'd been in too much of a hurry to even think of getting them off. Her legs were spread, her thighs reddened—probably from his beard stubble. Hell, he should have shaved, but he'd been too on edge to think about much of anything before she'd shown up. And after? Well, thinking had been pretty much impossible. He'd need blood flow to his brain for that. He could see the flesh between was flushed pink and swollen, glistening with her cum. Man, he'd done that. She looked liked she'd been well and truly fucked. He frowned. No, that wasn't exactly right. With her spectacular body totally relaxed, her hair tangled and fanned out across the sheet and her eyes heavy lidded, she looked like she'd been thoroughly…pleasured. Yeah, pleasured.

Sam had never been much into kissing after sex. It was kind of beside the point, but he suddenly wanted inside of her again, even if it was just his tongue in her mouth. He cupped a smooth cheek, holding her still while he lowered his mouth to hers. He felt the jolt to his gut as he slid his tongue across her lower lip and into her mouth. He groaned when their tongues touched, swallowing her sigh and the moan that sounded like it was torn from her. He threaded his fingers into her hair and angled her head a little more, slanting his mouth more firmly against hers and sank into it, into her, in a kiss that had his dick hard and aching again in an instant. He wanted her under him again. Hell, if the images he had in his brain were any indication, it was going to take most of the night just to try all the positions he was imagining. He'd come and he rarely went for a repeat performance once the initial appeal had been satisfied, so what the hell was going on? What was it about this woman that he couldn't seem to get enough of her?

* * * * *

Jillian's first thought was that it really was huge. She'd known it was large, of course she did, but didn't remember it being *this* big. But then she'd never actually seen it finished, and it had been a long time ago. Once she'd completed the sittings and gotten her money, she'd been so out of there. Her second thought was that *it really was her,* in all her naked glory. She sat amid rumpled white sheets, her arms wrapped loosely around her drawn-up knees. The pose would have been almost coy if not for the fact her legs were angled slightly to the side and the observer had a clear and very explicit view of the folds between her legs and one softly rounded, pink-tipped breast. The room in the painting was shadowed, but there was enough light to see every detail between her legs. Her head was bent, her hair tousled and trailing down the curve of her back and over one arm. Her face… God, her face was turned slightly away, but her eyes stared straight out of the painting as if they were inviting the viewer to join her. She was pretty sure she'd never looked like that before in her life.

"The resemblance is amazing."

Jillian jumped as Sam sauntered slowly into the room, a room she assumed was his bedroom. She'd woken alone in the room where they'd fallen asleep together a few hours ago and had gone looking for him, following the sound of the shower. She'd been going to join him. Instead, she'd found *this*. In the dim light, she'd almost missed it.

She pulled the edges of his shirt more closely around her. She'd grabbed it from the floor and hadn't bothered to button it. The soft, wrinkled cotton still held traces of his scent. She could have used the confidence that came with knowing she looked good, but her hair was probably a bird's nest, her makeup long gone and she still felt wet, sticky and achy between her legs.

Sam's hair was damp and ruffled where he'd probably made a token effort to dry it and the odd droplet of water clung to the smooth skin of his shoulders. A snowy white towel was wrapped around his waist and he smelled of some tangy, citrusy soap. It was clean and very, very male. She knew she must look like crap. Who gave *him* the right to look so goddamn gorgeous?

He was watching her warily. And so he should.

"You," she breathed. "You're the one who bought it."

"Jesus, so it *is* you."

Jillian swallowed the lump in her throat and looked back to the painting. "Yeah."

"You know it's named for you?"

"Yes." *Jillian.* She hadn't given much thought at the time to what the finished piece would be called. When she'd found out it had just made the risk of discovery one day that much more real.

"When I noticed you yesterday in the lobby it shocked the hell out of me. You want to tell me why a corporate financial whiz, a bright career in front of her, poses nude for a well-known artist? I mean, I assume you posed, unless you knew the guy."

"He wasn't so well-known at the time." Her voice was flat.

"Jillian," he said softly.

"I—I needed money when I was in college. I didn't have a cushy scholarship or a trust fund. I was studying for final exams. I was almost done, but I was about to be evicted from my apartment." Jillian wrapped her arms firmly around herself and took a deep breath. "I couldn't ask my parents for more money, my dad was already working two jobs. I had my student loans. And then I met this guy, a painter. He offered me what I thought was a fortune to sit for him. It was stupid I know, and it could have turned out badly, but…I posed for him. It seemed a fair exchange at the time." Jillian walked closer on shaky legs until she stood right in front of it. "I didn't know anything about art, but even I could see how good he was. It was probably only a total of ten hours or so. I never saw the painting actually finished. Until now."

"It's magnificent."

She caught the awe in his tone, but he wasn't looking at the painting. His gaze was centered on her. "It's an embarrassment," she fired back. "A big, fat regret. Something I always knew would come back to bite me on the ass someday."

She pushed the tangled hair back from her face and suddenly felt weepy, her throat tight and aching. "No wonder you didn't bring me in here."

"Jillian, I—"

"I knew you were a player, Sam. I got it loud and clear it was a one-night thing, but *this?* You have the gall to bring me here and fu-fuck me, knowing you have *this* here?"

"Jillian—"

"So, you saw me yesterday, put two and two together and decided you couldn't pass up an opportunity to 'do' the real thing? Is that what it was?" She waved her hand back toward the guest room.

"*That* was the fuck of the century." He ran both hands through the damp strands of his dark hair. "Okay, I admit I've been obsessed with it since the first time I saw it and it's interfering with my sex life. I took one look at you and I had to have you. I'd already fucked you in my head, over and over, in every way you can imagine. You know how many times I've lain here jerking off to it, even after I've fucked some chick's brains out?"

Yeah, brilliant move, Steele. Tell her outright you're some kind of pervert along with being an unfeeling pig.

"So what was earlier? An exorcism?"

Sam winced at the look of hurt on her beautiful features and the sound of her voice. He got the disgust and the anger and accepted them, yet it was the hurt and the sound of unshed tears in her words that tore through him.

"Look, Jillian, I'm captivated by you. Yeah, captivated, and if you knew me better you'd know that's not a word normally found in my vocabulary."

"The painting—"

"It's not that. It's you. I think that's maybe why I was drawn to it, *because* it was you."

"Yeah? Except you didn't know me then."

How did he explain it when he couldn't, not even to himself?

"Sell it to me."

He frowned. "What? Do you have any idea how much I paid for it?"

"I know to the dollar."

"Then you know you can't afford it. Besides, it's not for sale. *Ever.*"

"Why?"

"Because..."

It's mine and I need it.

He'd bought the house because of the view of the ocean from this room. He wasn't about to admit he'd rearranged all of his furniture in here so that he could look at the painting of her while he was lying in bed, and to hell with the incredible view. That should have given him some clue.

"So, you were just working some fixation you've developed out of your system?"

For weeks Sam hadn't been able to get off without picturing the painting, fantasizing about sinking into the woman who seemed to taunt him from its depths, visualizing himself fucking her wildly out of control. Now that he had for real? It hadn't done a thing to lessen the lust, the need that ate at him. He just wanted her all the more. *Her.* Not the painting. It didn't have a thing to do with the fucking painting. He hadn't thought about the damn thing like that *once* since he'd seen Jillian yesterday. So, where did that leave him and what the hell did he do now?

She turned away from him. It gave him some respite from seeing the pain in her eyes, but he hated that she was already distancing herself from him.

The sex had been out of this world, just like he'd known it would be, even for someone of his experience.

So, how the fuck had it all gone to hell so fast? And how did he fix it?

Sam's silence was more telling than anything else. Jillian felt the pressure in her chest and the stinging sensation in the back of her throat that she absolutely refused to give into. She wouldn't give the bastard the satisfaction.

Even now her body felt the echo of what it'd felt like to have him inside her, holding her, kissing her. It'd been incredible, she'd really felt a connection with him. And him? It had been what? A chance for him to fuck his fantasy in the flesh? An added bonus for the fortune he'd shelled out for it? A chance to see if she delivered on the promise explicit in her gaze in the painting?

"Outstanding," she drawled, knowing she sounded bitter, but what the hell? "I hope I lived up to your expectations."

She needed to get away from him. She had such lousy taste in men. She went for the hot guys and they always turned out to be selfish assholes. Why couldn't she fall for a boring guy who'd treat her like a queen? Jeez, she'd settle for one not stomping on her heart as he screwed her over. It'd make a nice change.

It was why she hadn't allowed herself to go this far with a guy in almost two years. But she'd thought what? That he'd felt the same tug she had, the same magnetic pull that had her acting totally out of character and agreeing to a one-night stand, just to be with him? That Mr. Playboy Extraordinaire would suddenly change his ways and fall madly for her? *Shit.* She knew better than to tell herself that drivel. It just didn't happen and she'd do well to remember it.

She walked out of the room. He didn't have the guts to admit it and she didn't even want to look at him anymore. She was going to grab her stuff and get out of here. Hopefully, he'd do the decent thing and just stay out of her way. She'd known what it was, he'd been more than clear and she'd accepted it. So why did she feel like she could shatter into a million tiny pieces anyway?

Chapter Four

Jillian started when the doorbell rang. All her visitors were supposed to be screened downstairs and announced before being allowed up. She groaned. She just wanted to stay holed up in her apartment for the weekend. She looked down at the loose sweats and frayed tank top. Any way you looked at it, she wasn't up for visitors.

Peering through the peephole, she frowned.

"I'm not expecting anything," she called through the door.

She watched the delivery man look down. "It's addressed to you, Miss. No mistake."

Jillian sighed and opened the door. The brown paper-wrapped package was large. The guy had to have struggled carrying it up here all by himself. By the shape of it, it looked just like, wait—

"What is it?"

"I just deliver them, Miss."

She frowned. "Who's it from?"

"Ah..."

"Me." Sam stepped into her line of sight.

"Sam." Jillian felt her heart jump at the sight of him and everything inside her roared to life. All week she'd hoped and prayed she wouldn't run into him at the office. Thankfully, she hadn't even caught so much as a glimpse of him. She hadn't had to pretend an indifference she'd practiced, because she knew now she never would have been able to pull it off.

She took a deep, shuddering breath. She'd never seen him dressed so casually before, not unless you counted a towel as casual dress. It wasn't fair. What the guy could do for a pair of worn jeans and a simple blue shirt. "What are you doing here?"

He motioned absently to the package, but his eyes didn't move from her. "I brought you a present."

"Sam," she sighed.

"Ask me in, Jillian."

After a brief hesitation she stepped aside, careful to make sure he didn't touch her as he strode past. Once she'd closed the door she didn't have anything to do with her hands, but clasp them together. She knew it telegraphed her unease but the way he was looking at her made her downright nervous. He'd propped the package against the wall of her entry and simply stood looking at her. She'd always loved her condo and considered it spacious, but his presence seemed to make the whole place just seem small and cramped.

She choked back what she'd been about to say to break the awkward silence when he stepped in front of her, ignoring any personal space conventions, and looked directly into her eyes.

"Jillian," he began, stopped and took a deep breath. "You make me tremble, you know that? No woman has ever been able to do that to me before."

She tried to ignore the hammering of her heart and the fluttering in her stomach at his nearness. "What are you doing here?"

"It's yours."

"What?"

"The painting. It's yours. No strings."

"Mine?" Jillian gasped.

"Yeah. Do whatever you want with it. Burn the fucking thing if you want. Slash it to ribbons. I don't care."

"You're *giving* me a painting worth—"

"Yeah."

"Why?"

"Because it's a piss-poor substitute," he ground out. "Because I want you. Just you. Even if I never see you again, never get the chance to touch you, be with you, I still wouldn't want it. Not anymore."

Jillian frowned. What did that mean exactly?

He rubbed a hand over his lower face. "Look, I've never had any problem getting women. I get turned down, sure, but I just move on to the next available, willing woman. No big deal, it doesn't mean anything. This is not going to do me any favors, but with every other woman since I got that painting I've tried to, I don't know, recreate you. I knew it'd gone too far once I realized I was choosing women because of their resemblance to you and I've never really gone for brunettes before. And when I was fucking them, in my bed, in front of the painting? I was positioning them so that I could look at you."

Jillian turned away. Just what she needed to hear—him and other women. Was he really that dense?

He grabbed her arm and swung her back to face him.

"Jillian, I'm just trying to make you understand, make you see that you're different. It's not just that you're a woman I'm hot for at the moment, it's you. I don't want to move on. I don't want anyone else. I want you. *You.*"

He swore when she just continued to look at him. "Christ, do you realize how sexually compatible we are? We just fit."

"So, we're matched sexually," Jillian agreed dryly. "We satisfy each other, so what? You want to keep sleeping together on the side, in secret? Is that it? Because we've already established you have a strict rule about that in the workplace, but I'm some *anomaly.*"

"No. *Fuck no.* Everyone will know you're mine. Look, I get bored easily. I don't even like it missionary, in fact I avoid it like the plague. But with you… God*damn* it." He waved his arm in the direction of the package. "I don't want her. *It.* I want *you* and not just for a night."

When she still didn't say anything he turned away, put his hands on his hips, and bowed his head. His posture screamed dejection. She'd never imagined he could look like that. He was always so arrogant, vital, commanding of everything around him.

"*Fuck,*" he muttered, as if to himself. "I've negotiated some of the most complex, sensitive acquisition deals. I've convinced, cajoled, sold myself out of tight spot after tight spot, yet I can't tell you how I feel."

"Feel? You're talking about *feelings*?"

He turned around and pinned her with a look so filled with heat it made her shiver.

"I didn't just fuck you with my body, Jillian. I made love to you with my mind too." He laughed. It was harsh and self-mocking. "A first for me." He ran the flat of his hand around the back of his neck. "Cut me some slack, okay? It took me awhile to figure it out. Hell, I never even knew sex could be like that."

Jillian swallowed. "I…I made love to you too, it wasn't just sex for me. I tried to tell myself it was but I guess I'm just not built that way. That's why it hurt so much to think you just saw me as this *object*."

He framed her face in his big hands and she felt the slight tremor that rippled through him.

"Shh. Jillian, I'm sorry, so sorry. I never meant to hurt you. I swear it. I was thinking with my dick and I'm probably too used to getting whatever I want where women are concerned. I mean it. I don't care if I never see that damn painting again. In fact, I'd prefer it. And I can't bear the thought of anyone else seeing you like that either. Ever since I saw it, it's like you were looking out at me, like you wanted *me*, that you were calling to *me* and me alone. I don't want for that to be for anyone else."

Jillian felt the sting of tears at the sincerity of his words and the expression of open longing on his face as he looked down at her. Together they were a lot more than she'd had from any other guy. She stepped into him, welcoming his heat and the shudder that rippled through him.

"I'm sorry," he whispered again as his big hands rested lightly on her hips, the touch almost tentative, as he eased her forward until their bodies brushed together.

She placed a finger to his mouth and traced the fullness of his lower lip slowly. He touched her fingertip with a hesitant flick of his tongue, and just like that heat seared through her and she gasped. She saw his eyes darken, his jaw clench. She watched, mesmerized, as he slowly lowered his mouth to hers until she couldn't keep her eyes open any longer. He nibbled and licked at her lips in slow deliberate movements and she grasped his shoulders when it made her so lightheaded she thought she might fall. She opened her mouth and his tongue immediately plunged inside, thrusting against hers in a familiar rhythm that had her body trembling, on fire, wet and aching in an instant.

Sam ran his mouth in a trail of wet, open kisses up the sensitive cord of her throat. He smiled to himself savagely when he heard the catch in her breath.

"You have any condoms here? I wasn't expecting to get lucky. I mean, I was hopeful. I was going to be happy if you would just talk to me, but damn, Jillian, I need you. N*ow*."

"Yeah, somewhere," she gasped when he tugged on her earlobe with his teeth.

It roared through him. The intensity of it was shocking, the reality of it even more so. *He was jealous*. The thought of her with another man was like broken glass thrusting and turning in his insides. He'd never been possessive over a woman before but he wanted Jillian all to himself.

"They're old," she added. "Very old. Do those things go out of date?"

It placated the beast. Some. "If they are, there's other stuff we can do. I've regretted all week not letting you finish, for selfishly wanting you under me that first time. Do you know how many times I've fantasized about you coming against my mouth and how often I've thought about coming in yours?"

* * * * *

Jillian was lying on her side facing the mirror with Sam behind her, pressed up against her length and buried so deep in her that she could barely breathe. Well the inability to breathe probably had more to do with what he'd been doing to her clit with his tongue for the last twenty minutes, but she didn't think she'd ever get used to the feeling of his fullness inside her. Her leg was up and back over his thigh giving them a clear view of where he was buried up to his balls inside her.

She groaned. God, the guy was inventive. He'd eagerly explored her condo while she'd tracked down the box of condoms, and had her mattress off the bed and onto the floor right in front of her full-length mirrored closet doors by the time she'd returned. The wicked look he'd sported was something she wouldn't forget anytime soon.

He flexed his hips and she gasped, fascinated by the sight of his heavy testicles swaying and brushing her sensitive skin as he moved. Jillian hesitated when she realized her hand was moving, drawn to where they were joined.

"Go on," he groaned. "Touch us."

Jillian reached down between her legs, feeling her own slickness and cupped his balls, kneading them gently as he began to thrust slowly and deeply in a rhythm that was sure to drive her out of her mind. She felt them tighten in her palm and he groaned hotly against her neck again.

"That feels good, sweetheart. Yeah, so fucking good."

He slid his hand down her abdomen, brushing the quivering curve until he reached the stretched, swollen flesh between her legs. He rubbed with his rough fingertips, spreading her moisture over and around her already sensitized clit. Jillian whimpered.

She shivered at the image in front of her. She'd never seen anything so graphic before. She couldn't keep her eyes from where they were joined, her gaze locked on his cock as it moved in and out of her in a slow, powerful rhythm. The condoms hadn't been old and she could just make out the edge of it each time he withdrew, glistening with her moisture.

And Sam was watching *her*. He wasn't looking at their reflection; he was looking down at her face. She raised a trembling hand up and back to touch his cheek and he finally raised his eyes to hers in the mirror. They were dark with lust, dazed with need, filled with awe. The thrusts of his body into hers didn't falter.

"Jillian," he breathed. "Look at you. You're so beautiful. I can't hold out much longer."

Jillian felt emotion clog her throat. One firm touch from those strong, blunt fingers and she was there, could only close her eyes, lean back into him and give herself over to him and the pleasure he wrought from her.

She barreled into the intense orgasm, aware of Sam's hoarse shout against her throat, his hot breath on her skin, the tightening of his arms around her. She gave herself to him with a certainty they shared more than their bodies. They shared a powerful need, a need for each other that transcended convention, a need neither had imagined existed before fate had brought them together.

The End

PAY UP

Dedication

To readers. My readers. Those who took a chance on a newbie and bought and read Picture This. You rocked my world!

Chapter One

"Yes, yes, Rio, yes…oh…*God*, yes…"

Not again.

Carly felt heat flare in her cheeks, not to mention the other parts of her body. It washed over and through her all at once, leaving her weak, her breathing unsteady, and just plain…hot.

What the hell did Rio do to get them to moan and scream and gasp that way? *She'd* never called out like that in the throes of passion or anywhere else for that matter. She was also pretty sure it wouldn't have been with that sense of utter abandon or lack of regard for who might hear her. And let's face it, she just wasn't that great an actress.

One of the reasons she'd bought her condo in this building was for its construction, *specifically* the interior concrete walls. It should have been impossible, but some freak design with the ventilation system meant…they had to be going at it up against the entry wall that backed directly to hers. Why hadn't that occurred to her? They'd barely made it past his front door before…

Whew.

Carly inhaled quickly at the sharp pull low in her abdomen. She swore she could hear a faint rhythmic thumping and muffled groans too, but it could just as easily be her imagination taking over. It didn't take much to have her picturing Rio's big body and what he was doing with it to get that kind of response. God, he'd be hot and sweaty, his body gleaming with exertion, his dark hair damp and sticking up where urgent hands had been buried in it, maybe holding on to him, urging him on. He'd have his shirt off, but maybe he'd been impatient, unfastening his pants just enough, having thrust them down roughly so he could—

She took a deep, shaky breath. She really, really needed to get a life. Unfortunately, she'd heard the whispers and giggles for a long time about how awesome Rio was in bed. About how built he was...*down there,* and about how he knew his way around a woman's body like few guys did. Hearing the evidence of it for the second time in a week didn't help.

Carly could feel how damp her panties were against the hot, aching flesh between her legs. She couldn't help the clench of her inner muscles when she heard a definite thud and more with the moaning.

They were still going at it?

She'd figured after that crescendo they'd be done. She sighed. Yeah, she'd heard about Rio's stamina as well.

How could she be hot and bothered and jealous as hell all at once? The hot and bothered she wasn't so surprised about. She only had to picture Rio shirtless and she was there. Hell, she only had to imagine his big hands, the sharp line of his jaw, the flash of his smile or his startling blue eyes and that was enough. The shockingly intense jealousy had sneaked up on her over time. And now? It was like acid burning through her veins at the thought of him and what he was doing with another woman, *to* another woman.

So, who did he have over there?

He hadn't dated anyone regularly since the woman he'd been seeing when they'd first met. He never lacked feminine attention though. Being a tall, dark-haired, ripped firefighter didn't hurt him in that department either, but he didn't play the field like he could. Sometimes he went weeks without seeing anyone. Not that she was keeping track or anything. Aw, jeez, who was she kidding? She knew every woman he'd ever gone out with. It was the second time this week with the sound effects and it was getting on her nerves, not to mention her libido. So, all right...she didn't have to stand in the kitchen, close to her front door where the sound seemed to be the loudest. She could have moved and spared herself, because she wasn't sure her heart could stand much more either, but something kept her rooted to the spot.

She closed her eyes and leaned back against the counter. Her body was on fire, her clothing rough against her overheated skin. Even the softness of her washed-to-death t-shirt seemed abrasive against her pebble-hard nipples. She gasped as the muscles between her legs and deep inside where she burned flexed involuntarily. Her panties were soaked.

Dammit.

It was inevitable. She knew, she just knew, before she went to sleep tonight she was going to be making good use of her vibrator, imagining it was Rio pleasuring her, his unforgiving tongue flickering over the swollen bud of her clitoris before his big body thrust in and out of her as he braced *her* up against the wall. She had to give in to it, there was no choice, because if she held out, the need and want and lust became unbearable. Been there, done that. Greg hadn't been able to satisfy that in her either. Despite how pleasant their sex, he couldn't satisfy the craving she had for Rio. He never had. She snorted. Yeah, thinking sex with him was "pleasant" should have given her more than a clue, a long time ago.

God. Rio Reyes. He'd been her sexy neighbor for just over a year, a good friend for almost the same amount of time and her secret crush since the day he'd helped her "de-wedge" her console table from the apartment elevator. An elevator she wasn't supposed to be using for moving in her furniture. He'd laughed at her with his infectious smile and gorgeous dimples and she'd been gone.

She sighed. Crush was such a lame word to describe the reaction she'd had to him at that first meeting and the *yearning* she'd felt ever since. She'd thought at first it'd been mutual. She would have sworn she hadn't imagined that spark when he'd laughed at her futile attempts to move her table, when he'd helped her carry it up to her new place, when he'd shaken her hand and introduced himself when he realized she was his new neighbor. The feel of his rough hand wrapped around hers had almost caused her to swoon at his feet and Carly wasn't the swooning type. The way he'd looked at her that day…it could still cause her to tremble. She'd learned later he was in a long-term relationship and although they'd eventually broken up, he'd never made a move on her, never shown the slightest interest in her that way.

Rio was nice. Just…nice. It might not sound very exciting, but along with being one of the hottest guys she'd ever seen, he was fun, easygoing, thoughtful and incredibly respectful, especially of women. He also watched his language around her and she'd always thought it was sweet. Add to all of that the fact he was one of San Diego's finest, and the combination was unusual and pretty much irresistible.

Damn, damn, damn.

Carly shoved the ice-cream carton she still held in her hands back into the freezer and slammed the door, wincing when it opened slightly again before finally closing. No way. *No way.* She wouldn't be a fucking stereotype, sitting home alone on a Friday night shoveling vanilla-bean ice cream down her throat and fantasizing about something that was completely out of her reach. So, she got dumped by her boyfriend today. Greg had actually dumped her. *So what?* It wasn't even that she was hurt all that much, but the jerk hadn't had the decency to give her an adequate reason. He hadn't even had the decency to do it in person, and she didn't need an audible reminder that she didn't have anyone to have wild monkey sex with. That the guy she *did* want to have sex with was giving it to someone else.

So yeah, she was mad. Good and mad. Because she'd had doubts about Greg for weeks, maybe months, and she should have been the one to end things. Because she'd never actually had *any* sex that would qualify as "wild monkey sex". *Ever.* Instead, she'd let things slide with Greg, thinking perhaps a less than perfect boyfriend was better than being alone.

Because then what would she do? Drool and fantasize about Rio, that's what. And what do you know? It'd been less than four hours and she knew she'd been right. *It sucked.*

* * * * *

"Come on, Carls."

Carly groaned into her pillow at the deep, rough voice. She'd barely been able to sleep after the show he'd put on last night and she was damn tired. In that moment, she regretted like hell the exchange of keys that meant he felt as if he could come in here anytime he chose. Okay, not really. She actually reveled in the sense of intimacy, no matter how false, that he was comfortable in her place. But did she really want to look into his satisfied face knowing what he'd been doing last night? Especially when *she* probably looked like crap?

"Rio, it's Saturday," she mumbled.

"So?"

"So, I just know it's some ungodly hour and I don't have to work today. Just because you have a weird schedule that doesn't take into account weekends, it doesn't mean—"

He muttered something too low to catch. "I don't have any patience for this routine today, Carly. Get your butt out of bed."

Carly lifted her head up from her pillow but could barely see him through the hair covering most of her face. She'd never heard that tone from him before, at least not when he was talking to her. And he never called her Carly. She pushed the tangled mess out of the way. He was standing by her bed, hands planted firmly on his hips, glaring. She tried not to let her focus land on his crotch, but it was an effort. It was right there in her line of sight.

"Jeez. You should be in a *much* better mood than this," she grumbled.

"Meaning?"

She buried her head back into her pillow so she didn't have to notice the way the fabric of his t-shirt stretched tautly across his broad chest, flat stomach and bunched around his hard, muscled biceps, but she'd caught his quick frown.

"Why are you torturing me like this?"

"Because you asked me to."

"I don't feel like it this morning. I'll run with you tomorrow. I promise. I had a lousy week at work and—"

"Come on. I'm ready to go."

Carly groaned, trying to burrow farther under the covers. She was so not a morning person. "Rio, seriously, I worked—"

He sighed. "No. You made me promise I wouldn't listen to you, no matter what you said, how you begged or what you offered, I was to ignore it. Now… Get. *Up*."

He yanked the covers off her and her cocoon of warmth was gone, just like that.

"Now, Carls."

Even spoken in a tone of complete exasperation, the shortened version of her name in his deep, rich tones brought shivers to her. It always did. No one called her that but him. She'd always been "Carly" to everyone and a few kids at school had made it "Carl" for a while, but his private name for her never failed to make her feel…special.

She sat up slowly and yawned. "Okay, okay, but I need to shower first."

"You're just going to get sweaty anyway," he sighed. "Just throw something on and let's go."

She knew she looked horrified. She could still feel the slight tenderness between her legs and wrinkled her nose. She felt swollen, hot and damp, *used* there. She'd all but collapsed into sleep once she'd almost run the batteries out on her vibe last night. No way was she going *anywhere* without showering.

As it was, she was going to have to run beside him, trying her damnedest not to check out his muscles and his… God, imagining just where his hands, his mouth and his...*cock* had been last night. The lance of pain was enough to quell the lust for a while, but it never lasted long.

Neither did the satisfaction she'd given herself last night. *Three times.* One look at him, especially in this close proximity, with loose drawstring pants sitting low on his lean hips, looking sexy and male and vital and she was right there again...wanting him and not being able to do a damn thing about it.

She dragged herself from the bed and walked toward her bathroom. She tried not to look at him. He was like the sun, compelling and hypnotic, and she knew it wasn't good for her to stare at him, but it was almost impossible not to.

"Give me five minutes."

She heard him sigh again before he said, "Hey, is that my shirt?"

Busted.

Carly stopped and turned around, trying to act casual. *Yeah, right.* As if she could pretend any such reaction around Rio, particularly in a room with a bed mere feet away, her toys tucked in her bedside table and her body still humming from a series of releases where he'd been front and center, fantasy-wise.

She'd completely forgotten what she had on, what she'd thrown on because nothing else was clean. The shirt was a ragged gray t-shirt Rio had left at her place months ago. Okay, so she might have snagged it out of his sports bag when he wasn't looking, but he had any number of t-shirts and this one wasn't that far from the rag heap. She'd figured he'd never miss it.

"Ah...it might be. Probably."

"Wondered where it had gotten to," he murmured. "I want it back, Carls."

"Sure."

Carly turned to make a hasty retreat to the bathroom. He'd never see the shirt again. No way was she about to relinquish it. It was dumb and probably seriously pathetic but it made her feel close to him, especially when the night was long and lonely as it'd been last night. She recognized on some level it was probably far from healthy, but if that was all she could have of him when she wanted him so bad she ached, then she'd just have to deal with it.

Right now.

Rio wanted to utter the demand to her retreating back, to throw caution to the wind and just say it. He told himself it was to see what her reaction would be, nothing more, but he really just wanted to know what was under it. *Bad.*

He felt as if he'd swallowed his tongue since he'd pulled those covers back. Her legs were killer. He already knew that, but seeing them like that, curled up against her, their tanned lengths looking like rich honey against the white sheets, the shirt bunched up around her hips and knowing she was probably naked beneath, or near enough to it... Well, he might just have a heart attack.

Did she sleep in panties? Tiny little scraps of nothing? Or was she bare-assed naked under that shirt? He could tell from the jiggle of her breasts she didn't wear a bra to bed. Seeing his shirt draped over her, its length skimming her bare thighs...*man,* it was just plain hot. He'd never seen a woman wear his stuff before. Sure as hell, if he'd slept all night with a woman like her, she wouldn't have woken up with a stitch on.

Carly looked like a golden beach babe with her sun-kissed skin, athletic build and her long, wavy hair. Even the light-brown color looked as if it were streaked with gold. No one looking at her would have guessed she was really a computer geek, a programmer with one of the banks in town. Guys always noticed her looks first and made dumbass assumptions about her. It pissed her off to no end, but who could blame them? She was gorgeous, sexy and...yeah, incredibly fuckable.

Rio shook his head in disgust. When the *hell* had he become obsessed with sex? Sure, he was a guy, he thought about sex a lot, but it was with a guy's normal sex drive or so he'd always thought. Lately… He inhaled deeply. *Christ*, even the room smelled like sex to him. Sex and warm woman.

He registered the sound of the shower running and groaned. Damn, that was all he needed. To imagine her naked body, all wet and slippery, her hands running over herself, across her breasts, between her legs, soapy rivers of suds running over the curves of her body.

Fuck.

He reached down and adjusted himself before she came back, gasping at the contact with his own flesh. It's a wonder she hadn't noticed the boner almost poking a hole in the front of his pants. How could she miss it? Even the snug boxers he'd taken to wearing didn't seem to be able to contain it this morning. The action he'd gotten last night should have more than taken the edge off. *Should have.* It obviously hadn't done shit. He flexed his hand. Jerking off didn't help either. He'd tried that. *Repeatedly.* All it did was improve the muscle definition in his right arm and piss him off to no end.

He should be shot. Carly was his friend, for fuck's sake. She trusted him and here he was…ogling her body, imagining what he'd like to do with it and generally acting like a damn pervert. Jesus, she had a boyfriend. The guy was a prick, but still, Carly was with someone else. Someone who had the right to touch her, sleep with her, do whatever the hell he wanted to her, whenever the hell he wanted. And that someone wasn't him. That was just reality and he needed to get with the program, because now he was fucking women because he was horny and they were available rather than being generally interested in them, and that made him feel like an asshole. He'd never been like that. He didn't know what he was going to do about this fixation he'd developed, but he knew he had to do something. And fast.

Carly felt pumped and alive, grateful as she always was that Rio had stood his ground and forced her to it. She watched him covertly as they stood cooling down. His hair was damp with sweat and he was breathing roughly, deeply. It was way too easy to imagine the sound of that rough breath sawing in and out hotly against her ear instead of into the cool air, maybe as he held her down with his big body stretched out over hers, as he licked at her earlobe, while he—

"I…ah, Carls… I won't be able to run with you anymore…for a while, anyway."

Carly took a deep breath and frowned. Rio ran his hand around the back of his neck. It wasn't a gesture she was familiar with from him, and in anyone else she would have said it was nerves.

He wasn't looking at her. In fact, he bent down and tied a shoe she was pretty sure was already tied. She knew she'd been surly and snarky all morning, out of sorts and in a downright bad mood but…

"Rio, morning's not exactly my best time. I—"

He shrugged. "Yeah, I…ah…I might work out with the guys for a while. Hit the gym instead, maybe."

He'd always said he hated the gym scene. It didn't sound convincing and it looked as if he knew it. She felt the dread settle in the pit of her stomach like lead.

"Rio, I'm sorry. *Really.* I was a bitch this morning. I just…"

She'd gone to bed last night feeling lonely, full of longing and mad as hell at Greg, at herself and at *him*. It didn't take a genius to figure she'd taken it out on him, and now…

"It's okay, I'm used to it."

Her stomach sank. God, had she really become *that* bad?

Carly attempted a smile she knew was weak at best. "My ass is going to get a mile wide without you pushing me to get out and run when it's the last thing I want to do."

"Your ass is your problem."

She inhaled sharply. It was harsh, especially coming from him.

"Sorry," he added. "It's got nothing to do with you. It's—I'm just going to mix it up, okay? I'll catch up with you on Friday."

For all her grumbling, Carly was pretty fit. She kept up with him. At least she'd always thought she had. Maybe he'd been humoring her the whole time?

It's not you, it's me. Yeah, where had she heard *that* before? Perhaps she was reading too much into it, but if he hadn't just blown her off, why did it feel as if he had?

Chapter Two

"I'm surprised you didn't cancel tonight. I heard what's-his-name's in town."

Carly's boyfriend traveled a lot with his job and usually didn't get back in town until late on Fridays. Not that he was keeping tabs on the prick or anything, but Rio knew he was around, so why was she still hanging out with him? If she was his, no way would he let her hang with another guy, even if it was pizza, beer and crappy TV. *Period.* And if that made him an old-fashioned, paranoid Neanderthal? Then bring it on.

Carly shrugged. "We're not together anymore."

Rio's senses went on full alert and his heartbeat kicked into high gear. "Since when?" he managed, but barely, lowering the beer bottle he'd been about to put to his lips.

Rio saw the shrug for what it was this time, a sorry attempt at "no big deal".

"Greg dumped me. He didn't even have the decency to do it in person. He just called me out of the blue last week and told me it was over. No reason—just that he was done."

Holy shit.

He'd really broken up with Carly? All he could think was...*what a fucking idiot.*

Rio hadn't seen her all week, not even coming or going in the corridor or the garage, and the hell of it was...he'd missed her like crazy. He'd become more than used to seeing her than he'd ever have guessed, but watching her prance around in those tiny shorts that hugged her ass cheeks and showcased her endless legs had become more than he could stand. Well, without causing him some serious injury and having Carly notice he had more than a friendly interest in her. She'd had a boyfriend. He'd reminded himself of it constantly, but lately it hadn't seemed to do any good. He didn't cheat and he didn't go after anyone else's woman, so the fact that he hadn't been able to rein in his interest or his body's reaction to it seriously pissed him off.

His date last Friday night had been beautiful and eager to please and oh so talented, and although he'd finally come, he hadn't been that into it by the end. The screaming and moaning had become annoying rather than a turn-on. He didn't mind snuggling up to a woman afterward, but he hadn't wanted to linger. In fact, he'd gotten her out of there as quickly as he could without seeming like a total jerk, but he'd still felt like an asshole. Jesus, he wasn't that kind of guy. He didn't want to be that kind of guy. And the worst part of it? He'd been thinking about Carly before, during and after. *Again*. And that just pissed him off even more.

"You don't seem too broken up by it," he offered.

"Not really, but I should have been the one to dump him, probably a long time ago."

"Yeah?"

"Yeah…I guess I let it linger for too long." Carly folded her long legs under her on the sofa and looked over to the windows and out into the night. "You know, it's just…"

Rio took a deep breath. He hated the faraway look. He thought the guy was a real piece of work, but he hated even more the thought of Carly upset or hurt by anything, least of all a guy like that.

"He was a jerk, Carls. Trust me. You can do better than that. A lot better."

Carly glanced back over at him sharply. "You never said anything."

He shrugged.

She wasn't the only one surprised. He'd promised himself he'd never say anything. The guy had called him on his lust for Carly whenever he'd gotten the chance. He'd never let an opportunity go by to goad him that he was fucking her and how. She didn't need to know some of the things he'd said about her, behind her back, to anyone who'd listen, but it had driven Rio crazy.

Carly was his best friend. It had happened over time and had surprised the hell out of him. It wasn't as if he'd never been friends with a woman before—he had—but he usually had them in his bed as well. This was different, even from what he'd had with Liz. It wasn't as it would be if she was a guy, but he talked to her about crap he never would have with another man. His level of crudeness might be toned down, but he loved hanging out with her. He felt relaxed and not at all like he was with other women. She could be sarcastic, sweet and funny and she made him as hot as hell.

The last part had become a problem. A big problem. And not just because of the boner he always had around her. For him and Carly, their timing had never been right. And now? Where the hell did that leave him?

Rio had shown up with pizza and beer, the kind Carly loved from a local micro-brewery and she knew he had to have stopped by there to pick it up himself. It was stuff like that that just made her fall for him all over again, each and every time. The thing was, she knew Greg would never have bothered and she doubted he could name any of her preferences anyway. Was it any wonder she hadn't been able to stop comparing them?

He was dressed in worn jeans and a soft-looking black faded t-shirt. It was loose but only emphasized the lean, hard body beneath. And God, those jeans—they should be illegal. The way he sat on the sofa, legs spread wide, well, she'd been trying not to stare at it—*him* all night. She'd never seen him naked but she'd checked out the bulge of his package, plenty of times. The soft jeans only seemed to enhance it, especially the way he was sitting. God, how often had she looked at him and wanted to have the freedom to trail her hand across the hardness of those arms, down his chest, to rest her hand against his abdomen, lift up his shirt and put her mouth to his warm skin? To use her tongue and try her best to make him moan? Whenever she wanted? Countless times. *Countless times* she would have given almost anything for the privilege.

She took a deep breath. She really just needed to learn how to suck it up or maybe move on completely. Problem was, she'd been sucking it up for a long time now and it wasn't exactly working for her. She'd thought about it before, cutting herself off from him completely, but had never been able to take it past the "oh crap, that's not an option" stage.

She reached to the coffee table for another slice of pizza. It was probably a dumb move considering Rio wouldn't be dragging her sorry ass up and out to work it off tomorrow.

"So anyway, what's Cole like?" she asked, hoping she didn't sound desperate to change the subject, but knowing he'd see through it if she did.

"Cole?"

"Yeah, what's he like?"

He frowned. "What does that mean?"

"You know, what kind of guy is he?"

Rio sat back and looked at her. "You want information from me so you can decide if you'll hit on the new guy at my work or let him hit on you, is that it?"

"*No*, I—"

"Didn't take long."

"What?"

"On the prowl already, Carls?"

"*No*. Jeez, what's *your* problem?"

He lifted his beer and drank deeply. "Maybe I'm horny."

Carly snorted. "Horny? You had the screamer over last week. *Twice*. How could you be *horny*?"

"What?"

Oh-ho.

"Ah… Yeah…I probably should have mentioned it to you before. The ventilation—I can sometimes hear—I mean I assume you were still in the entry and…"

Rio glanced over to her entry area and up to the vent high on the wall.

"*Shit.* You heard that?"

"It sounded pretty loud so—"

"Yeah, I'm probably going to be deaf in one ear for another week. I'm sorry, Carls, I had no idea."

He didn't sound that embarrassed. Or that impressed.

"So, she doesn't rate a repeat performance?"

He glanced at her quickly, surprised by the question. "God, *no*."

"Then what did you see in her in the first place? I mean, I assume it was her both times last week, unless—"

"*Christ*…yeah it was the same woman."

"So?"

"So…drop it."

"But I'd really like to know—"

"Yeah, but then you're not a guy."

"*So*?"

Carly couldn't help pushing it. What the hell did a guy see in a woman enough to sleep with her *twice*, but not want to take it any further?

He sighed. "Let's just say that apart from a killer bod, she could suck golf balls through a hose and leave it at that, okay?"

It was sharp, intense, the lance of pain. It was all she could do not to gasp out loud. God, hearing him talk about allowing another woman those liberties with his body, touching him, taking him in her mouth, giving him that kind of pleasure…it *hurt*.

She tried to ignore the ache deep in her chest and took a bite of the limp pizza she still held in her hand. The last thing she wanted was to put food in a stomach that was churning, but it was something to do with her hands and could probably disguise the sudden tears she felt at the back of her throat.

"So why not a repeat performance?"

He sighed. "I'm done for a while. I'm just…done."

Rio leaned forward, his elbows on his thighs. He looked at her with heavy-lidded eyes as she chewed.

"Enough with *my* sex life. What about you?"

"*Me*? I don't officially have one right now, a sex life that is."

His look turned intense. "Well, when you do…do you do anal?"

"What?" Carly coughed, almost choking on the pizza she hadn't been able to swallow.

"Do you?"

She frowned. She'd let the horny comment slide, but *this*?

"Rio, what's come over you?"

"Just making conversation."

"Well, then maybe you need to go talk to someone else."

He shrugged and looked down between his spread legs, twirling the beer bottle between his hands. "Have you? Do you?"

She wasn't used to such explicit talk from Rio, in fact, he couldn't have surprised her more if he'd stood up and stripped in front of her. She knew which she'd prefer. Carly should have told him to go to hell, it's what she would have said to anyone else who talked to her like that, but there was something almost…vulnerable in the line of his jaw as he looked away from her.

"I…all right. No. I haven't. That requires a lot of trust and I…haven't been there with anyone yet, you know?"

When he only nodded, she said, "What about you?"

He shrugged. "A few times. It's not something I think about much."

Yeah? Then why did he ask me about it?

* * * * *

"It sounds like a stripper's name," Carly scoffed. They'd cleaned up the remains of dinner and dumped the movie Rio had also shown up with in favor of a re-run of some reality TV show. It was barely marginal on the watchable meter, but it was some welcome light relief. Very welcome.

"It's not a stripper name."

"Sure it is," she insisted.

He smiled, his dimples making an appearance along with the belly tug she got at the sight of them.

"Yeah? Know a lot of strippers, do you?" he challenged.

"Probably every second one of them is called Honey."

"Sorry, Carls," he laughed. "But you don't know what you're talking about."

"Really? Been to a lot of strip joints, have you?"

Rio shook his head, his gaze swinging around to rest on her. "If I'm interested enough in a woman to want to see her naked, I want to be the only one looking."

Oh boy. Why did that have to sound so damn hot?

Carly swallowed. "I bet if I went down to the Pink Pony right now, there'd be at least one stripper working with that name."

He frowned. "What the hell do you know about the Pink Pony?"

Carly rolled her eyes. "Please."

When she didn't say anything else he added, "No one named Honey works there."

Carly lifted her chin at his superior tone. "Yeah? Wanna put your money where your mouth is?"

"I don't want your money."

"Okay, then what?"

Everything inside him stilled at the image that slammed into him. Carly, naked, her hair all mussed, stretched out in front of him on a big bed in abandon, spreading her gorgeous legs for him in silent invitation.

He stretched out his leg, trying to give himself some much-needed room. His jeans suddenly felt as if they were doing their best to strangle him.

"We're both single, right?"

"Ah, yeah..."

"Then let's make this really interesting. A...favor. Winner's choice."

She frowned. "A favor?"

"Yeah. A sexual favor."

"Ah...I..."

What the hell is he doing?

He'd clearly shocked the hell out of her. He saw the uncertainty, the confusion. It looked adorable on her, but he could have kicked himself. He couldn't blame it on the beer. He'd barely touched his. He'd been pushing it all night, he'd known it, but hadn't been able to rein it in. And he'd just crossed a hell of a line.

He shook his head. "Forget it. I—"

"No. I...all right."

Rio felt his cock twitch, lengthen. Just like that he was so hard it almost hurt to breathe. His mind was suddenly crowded with visuals, reviewing and discarding possibilities, scenarios. *Shit.* He thought about everything when it came to her. He couldn't very well tell her he'd been fantasizing about her letting him do whatever he wanted to her, however he wanted it.

"You're on. It's moot anyway because I know I won't lose," she added.

Rio smiled savagely to himself. That was what she thought. It might not be what he'd pick, but whatever she chose as her favor still made him the fucking winner.

*****

"Hey," Carly said sharply when the quick hand brushed against the curve of her breast. *Again.* The first time he'd done it, she'd ignored him and given him the benefit of the doubt. This time it was clear he'd felt her up as he tagged her, on purpose and with no effort to hide it.

The jerk just shrugged and smiled at her. He was good-looking in a blond, slim, pretty-boy way—almost the complete opposite of Rio's dark, leanly muscled frame. The smile was mostly teeth and made her almost cringe when he looked her up and down.

It was a standing match after work. Same time, same place each week and anyone could play. She couldn't remember his name, but he'd joined their flag football game a time or two before. All she knew was that he'd leered at her those times as well.

"Keep your hands to yourself," Rio called from the other side of the marked-off field.

Carly smiled. She should have known nothing would get past Rio's notice. She looked across at him, expecting a quick smile in return, but he was frowning, his mouth a harsh slash in his tanned face. She could almost feel the tension emanating from him as the jerk gave Rio the bird and took his position again for the next play.

Carly gritted her teeth when she felt the brush again several minutes later, this time against the curve of a buttock. She hadn't even handled the ball that time. Before she even had a chance to round on the guy, Rio was right up in his face.

The hairs on the back of her neck lifted in warning.

"Rio, it's okay."

He ignored her. "I said keep your fucking hands to yourself."

Carly gasped. She'd rarely heard Rio swear hardcore, but it wasn't just the language. She'd never heard that tone of savagery from him before or seen the aggression evident in every line of his tensed body.

The guy smiled the slimy smile again and held up his hands. "Hey, no harm, man. It was just an accident."

"Once is an accident. Three times is a death wish."

She glanced at him quickly. She shouldn't have been surprised he'd noticed the first "accident" as well. Carly moved in front of Rio and put a hand on his chest as he took a step closer to the clueless jerk. He was hot to the touch, his shirt a little damp, his breathing harsh. He played tag football like he did everything—flat-out and with everything in him. He was as hard as stone and probably just as immoveable. And she knew. She just knew. He wasn't backing down unless he wanted to.

"Rio, it's fine." She tried to placate him again.

Carly released her breath slowly when she felt Rio's muscles relax marginally. If she hadn't had her palm on his chest, she never would have detected it from the stance of his body or the almost feral look in his eyes.

"Hey, nice camel toe, Carly."

Carly gasped. The jerk had already turned to leave with that parting comment, but Rio still surged forward, nudging her out of the way as he grabbed at the other man and swung him around with a tight fist buried in his shirt. He snarled something she couldn't catch and hit him with a vicious punch so fast, it was a blur.

He fell to the ground, clutching his nose and mouth, blood everywhere. God, she'd never seen Rio like this. He was usually so mild mannered, easygoing, so in control, yet at the moment he reminded her of a snarling, wild animal.

"I'll sue," the jerk warned, using his t-shirt to wipe his face as he gingerly stood, watching Rio warily.

Rio smiled as he flexed his fist. It was a smile she'd never seen from him before, threatening and full of menace. "Bring it on, asshole."

"You gonna beat up every guy who looks at her, Reyes?"

Carly looked over at Cole as he walked up. Despite his easy saunter and the pure mischief in his eyes, she knew he was ready to step in if he needed to. He'd joined Rio's crew about three months earlier and had seemed to fit seamlessly into the clique the guys had.

"He did more than look," Rio snapped, flexing his hand again, his glare fixed to the back of the quickly departing figure.

Carly frowned at Cole. "What are you talking about?"

The look Rio threw at Cole had warning written all over it.

"Man, she doesn't know?" Cole whistled. "Sucks to be you."

Carly looked from one to the other. "What don't I know? *What* are you talking about? Rio?"

He finally turned his head. His jaw clenched as his dark eyes swept across her face, down to her toes and back up.

"Don't wear those fucking shorts down here again."

Carly gasped. "*What*?"

"Every guy out here can practically see the cheeks of your ass."

"What?" Carly frowned, her initial shock giving way to a simmer of anger. "That's bull, but so what if it is? Does that give him the right to cop a feel? Rio—"

"Of course not. It's just..." He broke off and looked around. "*Fuck,*" he muttered, obviously realizing what she just did. They were the center of attention. Everyone was standing on the field, watching them, and no one was making any attempt to hide their curiosity. Cole stood with arms across his chest, not even trying to pretend he wasn't listening or interested.

"Rio." Carly frowned, but he'd already turned and walked off. "What's the matter with you?" she called out.

He didn't answer, just kept going. She watched as he jerked up his bag and sweatshirt lying on the ground by the field and just kept going, without so much as a backward glance.

Carly wanted Rio back. The Rio she knew wouldn't have lost his cool, would have calmly but forcefully told the guy to get lost and he would never, ever speak to her that way. He wouldn't have nixed their workout sessions. He wouldn't have talked to her about sex so explicitly or thrown out the suggestive bet either. He was acting so out of character lately and she had the sinking feeling she was losing him, or as much of him as she'd ever had anyway. She'd wondered if it would be better to cut herself off from him completely. Be careful what you wish for, right? She felt the sting at the back of her throat and swallowed it back with an effort.

She looked down at what she was wearing. She'd worn these shorts countless times, playing football and jogging with Rio.

She looked up at Cole. "Are they really that short?"

God, her voice sounded as if she were on the verge of tears and she hated that.

His smile was gentle. "Nah. You look sexy and they make your ass look hot, but they're not indecent. All the guys check you out. Why wouldn't we? We don't mean anything disrespectful by it and we don't think it gives us the right to do anything about it. We all know Rio would go apeshit anyway."

Carly swallowed. "So, what's up with him? Is there something going on at work?"

Cole just shook his head. "You'll have to ask him."

Chapter Three

"So, why here? What happened to Duffy's?"

Carly looked around the bar. It was smaller, had more of a younger crowd and just didn't have the same laid-back feel of their typical hangout.

One of the guys from Rio's crew laughed. "Reyes can't go back there. He's banned."

"*Banned*? For what?"

"Fighting."

Carly frowned. "*Fighting*? *Rio*? Are you sure?"

All at once the guy seemed uncomfortable, looked around at the group they were standing with and refused to meet her eyes. "Ah…you'll have to ask Rio."

"Well, he's not here right now."

"Right." The burly guy scratched his head. "Ah, Greg…your ex now, right? Rio…might have…beat the crap out of him for shooting his mouth off about you."

"*What?*"

"I wasn't there, but from what I heard, the guy more than deserved it."

Rio had fought with Greg? Had beaten him up? What the hell? She looked around just as Rio stepped behind her. He had to have heard the whole thing.

He shot a poison glare at his friend and leaned down to her.

"Christ, Carls, he was telling whatever dickhead who would listen how you let him fuck you in the ass."

His tone was low. She doubted anyone else had heard him.

"*What*?" The word came out a strangled gasp.

He shook his head and she frowned.

"You never said anything."

"You didn't have to know what a slimeball he was, but when he started talking about you like that, I…"

He broke off and ran a hand through the dark strands of his hair.

"So you *hit* him?" God, she still couldn't believe it. "Did you hurt him?"

"I sure as hell hope so."

"*Rio*."

"What would you have me do? Pull up a seat? The things he said… I couldn't let it go. I— He shut up, at least."

* * * * *

"Hey, Cole, how's it going? How you settling in?"

Rio sat down next to the other guy, but his gaze was glued to Carly across the bar. He had no idea what she was thinking. She hadn't said a word. Had just looked at him as if she didn't know him anymore and walked off. *Jesus.* He hadn't ever been going to tell her. He figured she'd never hear it from Greg. The jerk wasn't about to tell Carly Rio had laid him out flat on his ass spouting what he now knew were lies. What a mess.

"So, is this my 'stay away from Carly' talk?"

Rio threw his attention back to Cole and frowned, his gut tightening. "What the fuck are you talking about?"

"So, are you doing her or what? There's a lot of speculation, my friend."

"Who?"

Cole smiled. "Carly. Carly Wagner."

God, the fucker was playing with him.

"She's a friend, man."

"So?"

Rio shrugged. He'd noticed the way the other man had checked out Carly's legs at the game. He'd done it before, but Rio had shrugged it off. She had a boyfriend, Cole was a guy and Carly's legs were killer. Who could blame him? Now it was different. She was single and Cole's interest at their last game had just riled him so much that when that loser had felt her up, he'd been primed to go off like dynamite.

"So, you don't mind if I take a shot tonight? I hear she's single."

Rio felt his hand clench on the beer bottle and took a swig from it so Cole wouldn't notice. Christ, he *had* been going to try to steer his interest away from Carly, but how the fuck had the discussion gone to hell and turned tables on him?

"She doesn't go for casual sex."

Cole looked him straight in the eye. "Maybe I'm not looking for a quick fuck."

Rio watched the guy look over to where Carly stood with her girls. Ever since he and Carly had connected, it had been a natural progression that had somehow merged Carly's group of friends with his own work buddies. They tended to hang out at the same place on most Saturday nights and the guys looked out for the girls, made sure no one was bothering them. They were usually just out for a good time, to have a few drinks and dance. The guys ran interference for them. It worked out for everyone so far. A few hookups had happened, but nothing too serious.

"She's nice. I like her. *A lot.* There could be something, you know?"

Panic seized him like a clenched fist in his insides. Cole was a good guy—hell, he was a great guy, and Rio could all too easily see Carly going for someone like him, really going for him, especially after Greg had bowed out. Suddenly the thought of her in a permanent relationship with a decent guy didn't sit well with him. It was some fucked-up logic, but somehow when she was with the asshole, he'd known it was only a matter of time before Carly realized he was a jerk. He'd known it wasn't really going to go anywhere. This was different entirely.

"She's hot and sweet, man," Cole added when he didn't say anything. "It's a lethal combination. You hold off much longer, someone's going to snatch her from under your nose and not just to bang for a while. Maybe for good."

Be cool.

Rio took a deep breath, tried to control his reaction at hearing Carly referred to in those terms, but tempered it with an effort. "You don't know what the hell you're talking about."

"You can't deny the way you look at her. Don't worry, I don't think anyone else notices, least of all her."

"You're way off base, man."

"You telling me I can take my best shot? That if I hit on her tonight, left with her, it wouldn't piss you off?"

Piss him off? The mere thought would burn his insides like acid.

As Cole got up and turned away toward Carly, Rio couldn't help the hand that grabbed on hard and swung the other man back toward him. "You'll stay the fuck away from her," he snarled before he could stop himself.

Cole laughed. *Laughed*. "Yep. They all warned me."

"Warned you about what? And who's *they*?"

"The guys. Said if I showed any interest in her, I'd get warned off."

"Well, she's off-limits."

Cole smiled. It was knowing and grated like hell on him. "Whatever, man. But some guys won't respect you enough to step aside while you try to decide what the fuck *you're* going to do."

When Rio didn't say anything, he added, "Seriously. You need to make your move or someone with less ethics than the rest of us will ignore your warnings and go for it anyway."

* * * * *

"Wildfires fueled by fierce desert winds continue to threaten scores of Southern California homes and have forced thousands of people to flee. One person so far has reportedly been killed and firefighters from the San Diego Fire-Rescue Department have been battling multiple fronts of the firestorm going on three days. With strong Santa Ana winds forecasted..."

The voice of the newscaster faded out as Carly focused on the images instead of the words. All she could see were the fierce, out-of-control flames hungrily licking at everything they came into contact with, the thick billowing smoke, the homes, in danger and so close to the fires, some of them already smoldering ruins of black debris. Rio was out in that, somewhere, risking his life, facing God knew what, battling what looked to be an impossible adversary. She'd caught snatches of the news at work all day. It was a busy time for her. Usually she loved what she did, flourished on the challenge of it all. She had two projects nearing completion and hadn't been able to focus worth a damn on any of it. And she'd been sitting in front of the TV ever since she'd gotten home. They were doing around-the-clock coverage and she'd missed dinner so long ago, her stomach had finally stopped protesting. She knew she was unlikely to catch a glimpse of him, but at least she'd hear if one of the firefighters got hurt. *Wouldn't she*?

She hadn't seen Rio since the weekend, and even then it had been awkward. He'd been friendly enough, but something was wrong and she hadn't really known what to say to him about Greg. He'd probably deserved it, but it seemed so out of character for Rio. They'd lost the sense of ease they'd always had together and already the emptiness was eating at her.

Carly was so focused on the TV, she jumped at the soft knock on the door, her stomach lurching. No one could get into the building unannounced. Her heart leapt when she looked through the peephole and quickly swung the door wide.

Rio's whole posture screamed exhaustion and he looked awful. His eyes were red-rimmed, he had a bruise on his cheek and he hadn't shaved for days. His jaw was dark with stubble, giving him more of a rugged look than usual. He had a bandage on his arm and despite the fact it was clear he'd showered recently from his damp hair, she could detect the faintest trace of smoke on him.

"Hey. I wasn't sure if you'd still be up. I just wanted to say thanks for taking care of my place, getting my mail and stuff."

His voice was hoarse and scratchy. She didn't know if it was because of the smoke he'd probably been exposed to or because he was so clearly exhausted.

He swayed a little unsteadily. "Rio, why don't you come in and—"

"Can't. I'm dead tired, Carls. I'm going straight to bed. I have to be up and out again in the morning."

"Have you eaten?"

God, he looked so lean, more so than usual, his face drawn with fatigue, his jeans hanging low on his slim hips.

He shook his head as if it were the last thing he'd thought about.

Carly grabbed his hand and pulled him into her apartment.

"Carls, I can't. I—"

"Rio, you need to eat. Come on. Give me ten minutes and I'll whip something up for you."

"Carls..."

She led him to the breakfast bar. "Sit."

She was conscious of his eyes on her as she quickly poured him a large glass of chilled milk. He lowered his big body onto the stool slowly, angling it so that he could also lean against the side of the wall, as if he needed the added support to hold himself up.

"Thanks."

Carly worked quickly, whipping up scrambled eggs, sprinkling in some ham and cheese as Rio demolished the milk. By the time he was done, she'd put a steaming mound of food in front of him. Her own stomach clenched, reminding her she hadn't eaten either, but her attention was all focused on Rio.

"It's bad, right? I've been watching it on the news."

Rio looked up, his eyes dark and solemn. He nodded slowly and then went back to shoveling the food. He must have been starved.

"Yeah, it's bad."

By the time he was done, his movements were slow and jerky. She'd never seen him like this, totally out of it, docile. Usually he was so alive and vibrant he pulsed with energy.

"What happened to your arm?"

He shrugged and pushed back from the stool. "It's just a scratch."

She'd never much thought about the risks he took on a regular basis. He'd invited her to watch a controlled burn once. She'd been more distracted at the time with how Rio looked in his gear, but she hadn't been able to escape the harsh realities on the news. The thought of him having to go back was more than unsettling, it was disturbing and scary. She didn't think she'd actually felt fear for another person before.

Carly grabbed for him when he stumbled getting up from the chair.

"Rio?"

"Sorry." He put his hand on the wall and shook his head as if to clear it.

"What's wrong? Are you okay?"

"Yeah, I... They shot me full of something before Cole drove me home. I—"

Cole had driven him home? Carly frowned. "A shot? For what?"

"Stitches I guess."

"*Stitches*?" Carly looked down at the stark white bandage on his forearm. "Jesus, Rio you've got stitches in your arm? How many?"

"Ah, twenty or so. It's nothing, it's just—"

"A scratch. Right. Come on," Carly urged, grabbing his other arm when he swayed on his feet. God, the realization he could have been badly injured, *had* been hurt, burned coldly through her, its pang sharp and biting. "You can spend the night here."

"Carls, I'm..."

"Yeah, so tired you can barely function and apparently drugged to the eyeballs. I got that, so you can stay here."

Where I can keep an eye on you. The thought of him alone, needing something in the night but being helpless wasn't something she wanted to dwell too much on.

"But..."

"Come on."

Carly used her one spare room as her office so she led him into her bedroom. God, she was leading him by the hand into her *bedroom* and he was meekly following. How often had she pictured *that*? Trust her to be doing it while he was barely aware of it.

She motioned to his arm. "Do you need to do anything for it?"

"Nah. I...ah...I still smell like smoke. I'll need another shower."

His words were slow, hesitant. Carly looked at the dazed look in his eyes, at the way he slowly blinked as if he were trying to focus on her and led him over to her bed.

"I don't think so. Why don't you just sit here and I'll...ah..."

Carly stumbled to a halt as he grabbed his t-shirt at the back of his neck and jerked the entire thing off in one rough move, exposing his smooth muscled chest. He yanked at the button on his jeans a few times before it popped open and her mouth went dry, her attention focused on the soft-looking line of hair that arrowed under his navel down into the opening of his jeans.

Oh God. He's getting naked. Without-any-clothes-on naked.

He grabbed the waistband of his jeans with both hands, the muscles in his arms bunching.

"Ah...I'll just run next door and get you a change of clothes."

Carly felt odd being in his bedroom. She'd been in his place before, but never this room. This was the room he dressed and undressed in, the room he slept in, the room he...*fucked* in. Well jeez, she assumed he didn't always have sex up against the wall of his entry.

What did he sleep in anyway? He didn't seem the pajama type. She quickly grabbed a pair of sweatpants, a t-shirt and opened and closed a couple of drawers until she found his underwear.

Oh God.

They were all black, snug boxer-style briefs. *Every single pair.* She laughed. Not a lot of imagination, but hey, he so didn't need any window dressing. They had to look incredible on him, so why would he mess with perfection, right?

She felt depraved as she fingered the soft fabric, imagining what the material cupped when he had them on. She'd never much gotten into going down on a guy but the urge she had to look at, touch and taste Rio almost made her tremble. She wanted to lick his length, suck on him, cup and lick his balls until he trembled against her. She wanted to kneel in front of him in submission, his hands in her hair, urging her on until she brought him to the brink. And then she'd start all over again. She'd never let a guy come in her mouth before either, but she knew she'd let Rio. God, she'd insist. Just the thought of it and she was hot, wet and aching with need. What would he say if she won that dumb bet and claimed her prize as a blowjob for him?

Carly hurried back to her place, not wanting to leave him for too long, but he was already in bed, his breathing deep and steady. His clothes and shoes were scattered next to the bed where he'd been standing when she'd hightailed it out of there, as if all he'd been able to do was drop them where he stood. He'd pulled the sheet roughly up over himself, but there was still plenty of skin on display, stretched tautly over powerful arms and shoulders. She approached him slowly, still trying to come to grips with the fact that Rio was actually in her bed, naked or near enough to it. Hurt, drugged, but in her bed regardless. As she reached over to straighten the covers, he put a hand over hers, trapping it against the hot skin of his chest.

"Thanks," he rasped.

"Ah, sure."

Her mouth went bone dry as he reached up and cupped a hand around the back of her neck, pulling her roughly down to him. Her heart felt as if it jumped in her chest as she inhaled the warm scent of his skin. And then he kissed her. Softly, gently, but it was full on the mouth.

Oh wow.

Carly put her hand to her lips when he eased back. She'd had other kisses, of course she had. Deeper kisses, more passionate kisses, but this one would stay with her for a long time to come. It hadn't been the kiss of a friend. There'd been tongue for one, not much, but enough to elevate it out of the realm of a casual peck between friends. And he'd licked along her bottom lip as he'd pulled back. As she looked down, his eyes were already closed and his hand lay back against the sheet. She could almost imagine it hadn't really happened. All except for the pulsing heat low in her belly and the tingling between her legs. Too bad he'd probably been completely out of it.

Chapter Four

Carly woke in a rush, gasping at the hot breath on her neck, her hips writhing helplessly against the bed and the hard fingers inside her, moving in and out in a rhythm that was—

Where the hell were her panties?

Her nightdress was bunched up around her waist. Her body was burning up, raging with heat, wet and almost stinging with need. Rio was nuzzling and licking and sucking on her neck and his hand—

Her heart hammered as a hair-roughened thigh slid urgently between hers. Her leg somehow ended up over his. Had he lifted it there or had she, to give him better access? She was completely open to him, but his fingers eased slowly from her body. She tried to stem the sob that rose up into her throat and concentrate on dragging in a much-needed gulp of air. Before she could do either, he'd groaned into her neck, put a hand down to guide himself and pushed inside her in one long sure stroke that took him all the way in.

Oh God.

He was hard and big. She was hot and slick and her body clenched around him of its own volition.

He groaned, his hot breath fanning her throat as he sucked the skin of her neck in a hot, openmouthed kiss she felt all the way to her toes and exploded with sensation in her already engorged clit.

"Oh yeah," he breathed, sending shudders through her entire body. "Feels good…so good."

"Rio," she sighed, feeling as if she were balanced on the edge of…something.

His cock flexed inside her, and then he slowly withdrew, almost all the way out, before thrusting back in slowly and oh so deep.

"Mmmm?"

Carly gasped and clutched at his hard shoulders. Her whole body was alive with sensations she'd never felt before, all radiating from the flesh between her legs stretched tightly around a cock that began driving in and out of her in a long, slow but relentless rhythm.

Despite how exhausted she knew he was, one big hand held her hip firmly, keeping her exactly where he wanted her, maximizing his ability to slide in and out at the angle he wanted. As he thrust against her, he stroked against her clit, right where she wanted it, exactly the way she needed it.

She bit her lip to prevent the low moan from escaping. Her heart thundered in her chest, the blood roared in her ears. How long had he been fingering her in her sleep? She tingled all over, trembled all over and all of a sudden she was close…really, really close.

Carly angled her head back so she could look at him. His eyes were closed. Oh God, did he even know—

"Carls," he groaned.

So, he did know it was her.

He rested his forehead against hers, breathed her name again and thrust deeply, a little harder than before, and just like that she went over.

She whimpered and closed her eyes, her lower body jerking against him as her orgasm rolled through her, so powerful it was all she could do to hold on and endure the intensity of feeling. She was usually quiet in her pleasure, but it was too strong, too unexpected and she couldn't hold it in any longer.

"Rio, Rio, yes, *yes…*"

She heard Rio groan, felt his hand flex on her hip and felt the jerk of his body against hers.

Carly tried hard to get her breathing under control. It was almost impossible. Rio was a heavy weight against her and she could still feel the aftershocks of her release against her sensitized clit every time he breathed. As they slowly leveled off, she could only think one thing.

She was no better than the screamer.

And he'd come inside her. Oh God, he'd come inside her. She'd never let any other guy do that before. Well, technically she hadn't actually *let* Rio, but she'd even refused with Greg. It had been an ongoing issue between them, one of many. And *she'd* come. Just...*come*...without any theatrics, extended abstinence, mega-stimulation or major fantasy on her part. It had been all Rio. All she'd been focused on was Rio, all she'd been able to feel was him and he'd managed to have her to the edge in an instant. Hell, he'd thrown her over effortlessly.

She usually had to concentrate hard to orgasm, really hard. Everything had to be right—the light in the room, the position, any noise, the angle and she usually had to be primed. No self-pleasure for a while leading up to the deed. She also usually had to imagine something, typically one of her favorite scenarios, of being dominated, of being seduced, of...God...even anything featuring Rio of late. It was one of the reasons she knew she was going to break it off with Greg. It was one thing to use a nameless fantasy to get off, it was another to imagine her sexy neighbor and friend when she was with someone else.

Carly released the silky strands of hair at the nape of his neck she hadn't been aware were clenched in her fist. She eased back to look at him.

His eyes were still closed. She eased herself slowly from under him, gasping when he slid from her body, and hurried into the bathroom. She shakily washed herself before wringing out another washcloth in warm water.

The view when she went back into her room stopped her in her tracks. He was on his back sprawled over most of the bed, his big, tanned body standing out starkly against the crisp white of her sheets. His limbs were lightly sprinkled with dark hair, his skin smooth over the curves and valleys of a leanly muscled body that looked as if it were carved from warm, rich wood.

What she wouldn't give to be able to run her hands over every inch of him, to use her mouth, her lips, her tongue. But it had happened so fast. All she'd had time for was to clutch those massive shoulders and just…feel.

Sated, he should have been soft and…smaller. Instead he still looked partially hard. His cock lay thick and long up against the firm skin of his torso, still wet and glistening. His heavy balls lay between muscular thighs amid a nest of dark, coarse-looking hair that she would have loved to trail her fingers through.

He was so very male and so gorgeous and he was in her bed. He'd been in her. *Finally.*

Carly approach slowly, not wanting to disturb him. She put the washcloth to him as gently as she could, wiping him carefully, jumping when he flexed beneath her hand.

Despite his relaxed form, strong fingers snagged her wrist when she tried to pull back. There was incredible strength there, yet his fingers held her loosely, his eyes barely open, still dazed, unseeing.

"Carls?" he murmured.

"Yes?" she whispered, holding her breath.

"You came, right?"

She smiled. She couldn't help it. In any other guy, she'd think it was simply ego. Not Rio. Even out of it, so tired he could barely keep his eyes open, whatever it was that was such an integral part of him still demanded he ensure he'd taken care of her.

"Oh yeah," she drawled, but he'd already closed his eyes, drifting back to sleep.

* * * * *

What the fuck had he done?

Rio swallowed as Carly sighed softly and turned her head toward him, almost as if she knew he was staring at her, had been for the last fifteen minutes. The feeling of dread he'd woken with still sat heavy in his gut. Actually, the longer he stood looking down at her, the worse it got.

She probably hated him, probably never wanted to see him again. Or she would. Why couldn't he have left it the hell alone? Why couldn't he have left *her* alone?

He'd been thinking with his goddamn dick, that's why. Yeah, he could use the excuse he'd been exhausted, so tired he'd been barely able to think, out of it on pain meds, but all that was just so much bullshit. He'd known on some level, his body had known and recognized her and it had just *wanted*. To the exclusion of everything else.

He took a deep breath. She'd held on to him. *Tight*. She'd been so wet, she'd sighed and groaned his name. *His* name. And she'd wiped him off afterward. God, just thinking about it almost buckled his knees. Would she have done any of that if he'd been forcing her?

He ran his hand through his hair, pleased for the deep throb in his arm. He welcomed the pain. It served him damned right.

The thing of it was he'd blown it. Big time. He'd finally had her in his arms, under him, he'd had the chance to look at her, touch her, kiss her, show her how much he wanted her and he'd done none of it. *Nada*. He'd come almost as soon as he'd gotten inside her like some selfish, inexperienced kid who didn't know jack and just wanted to get off. He hadn't even thought to protect her. God, she'd been worried about him and he'd…he'd taken advantage of her. He'd thrown away everything. *Everything*.

It was an effort to tear his gaze away to glance down at his watch. *Fuck*, he really had to go. He knelt by the side of the bed, ignoring the tremor in his hand as he fingered a smooth strand of her hair. She looked so pretty in the soft light. He'd never noticed before how long her lashes were or that she had a sprinkle of small freckles across her nose. His stomach clenched at the thought this might be the last chance he'd ever get to be this close to her, to see how smooth her skin was, to inhale the sweet smell of her hair. Because next time he saw her? She was likely to tell him to go to hell.

Yeah, he'd fucked it all up royally.

* * * * *

The music was too loud. Her new boots were pinching her toes. Her drink was way too strong and the bar was just too damn busy. She was seriously going to scream if she got jostled one more time.

With all the bodies piled in here she shouldn't have had a direct view of Rio two tables away, but she did. And it was one she could have done without. She didn't need this. Not now that he'd kissed her and touched her and been inside her. The thought of him sharing his body with someone else after that… It felt as if a knife were slicing through flesh already torn ragged. As did the realization that he didn't seem to remember what had happened between them.

He'd been gone by the time she'd woken up that next morning. Two weeks. *Two weeks* and he hadn't said a word, hadn't given any indication that he recalled any of it.

Figures. She finally had sex with the hottest guy she'd ever known, one she'd lusted after *forever,* and he'd probably slept through the whole thing. And now, here she was with a front row seat as she watched Rio in action. *With someone else.*

And that smile. The flash of white teeth against the tanned skin of his face, the one that lit up his eyes and had the ability to send a sharp tug to the pit of her stomach every single time, except this time he wasn't even looking at her. He was directing it to a cute brunette who had an ass showcased by the tightest pair of jeans she'd ever seen.

"I see you're still panting after him."

Carly groaned. Just what she needed. Rio's ex and another reminder Rio preferred other women over her.

"I...ah, Liz. How are you?"

She looked as stunning as she always did. She was one of those women who were always immaculately dressed, didn't matter the venue or the time of day. She was perfectly made up and looked gorgeous in her probably silk black wraparound dress, showcasing just enough of her amazing cleavage for it to look classy. Carly tried hard not to feel dowdy in comparison but quickly lost the battle. Jeans, boots and a sexy green halter top had seemed perfect for the casual bar with a big group of her and Rio's friends. *Had*. Up until...now.

"You know, he's still the best lover I've ever had...gentle, thorough and oh so inventive. Trust me. I've tried hard over the last year to replace him. He's one of a kind."

Oh God, someone really wanted to torture her.

"You sound as if you're still stuck on him," Carly somehow managed.

Liz sighed and looked over to Rio. "Yeah, maybe, but not the way you mean. I loved the way he treated me, the way it made me feel, but I didn't love *him*, not really. I came to realize that when we split. Even now, after I was such a bitch to him when it was obvious he wanted to end it, I know he'd go out of his way to help me if I needed him. It's rare in a guy as hot as him, you know?"

Carly winced inside as Rio laughed at something the brunette said. "Yeah, I know."

"Besides, with Rio, when something's over, it's over. He'd never be interested in me again, not like that, which is why I was intrigued when he asked me down here."

Carly frowned and glanced back at Liz. "Rio asked you to meet him here?"

"He said there's someone he wants to introduce me to." Liz cocked her head to the side. "You know, I always thought he might have a thing for you. With me out of the picture, I thought…"

"Yeah, right."

"No seriously. To be honest, I… I was always kind of jealous of you. He talked about you all the time. He's never made a move on you?"

Liz had been jealous? Of *her*?

"No."

Well, not when he was conscious, anyway.

"Well, I'll see you around."

Not if she could help it.

"Yeah, sure."

Carly watched as Liz walked over to Rio, finally turning away when he smiled, leaned down and kissed her cheek. They'd been lovers, they'd explored each other's bodies, they'd slept together… God, just thinking about the things they must have shared, the things he'd done to her, what he'd let her do to *him*. Did she *really* need to torture herself anymore?

She no longer had the same ease with Rio that she'd always just taken for granted and she hated it. *Hated* it. Who would ever have thought she'd want it to go back to the way it was? Exactly the way it was. Just friends. She just wanted it back, she wanted *him* back. The killer of it was, he'd never really been hers, not really, not in any way that mattered.

She felt the tears that were never far away sting the back of her throat and blinked rapidly when everything blurred in front of her. Enough was enough. She'd had enough. She put her almost full drink down on the nearest available surface and pushed her way through the crush of people toward the exit. The snippets of conversation and laughter she caught along the way only seemed to mock her.

She let out a breath when she finally saw the door, eager for the quiet and the crisp, fresh air she knew was beyond.

"Hey, Carls, where—"

She glanced at Rio, sharply surprised he'd noticed her escape. "I'm leaving."

She saw the quick frown. "Why? We just got here. I saw you talking to Liz. She didn't say or do anything to upset you, did she?"

No, you managed to do that all on your own.

She shook her head. God, she just wanted to crawl into a tiny ball in the comfort of her own bed, wrap her arms around herself and cry, just let it all go. She didn't think she could hold it together much longer.

"I just need to get out of here," she rasped, her voice sounding odd, even to her.

"Are you feeling all right?"

Only if you consider a ripped and bleeding heart feeling all right.

"Fine. I'm fine. I just need to leave."

"Okay, I'll take you."

"Don't bother. It's just a few blocks."

He frowned and grasped her arm lightly as she turned back away from him.

Carly looked down at his arm. Even though he was wearing a long-sleeved navy shirt, she could still clearly picture the ragged scar that made her sick to her stomach every time she saw it, thought of the danger he regularly faced. It also served as a mocking reminder that while she might treasure every word, every second of that night, he didn't even know he'd touched her, held her, been inside her.

"You can't walk by yourself. It's dangerous and—"

"Oh, for God's sake. Just go back to your—*what's her name*—and…"

"Who? Carly, what's wrong?"

I'm jealous, you moron!

She almost yelled it at him. Almost, but she caught herself in time.

"Me?" she asked instead and shrugged his arm off. Was he really that clueless or was she just a much better actress than she'd ever given herself credit for? Carly looked around the crowed bar. Any number of Rio's buddies would be better than trying to pretend everything was still good between them and it would satisfy his protective streak.

"Fine, but I'll get someone else to walk me back."

"Like hell you will."

Carly turned for the door. "I'm leaving. I'm just…leaving."

He grabbed her arm again. "If you think I'm going to let you just walk out of—"

"Let me? *Let me*? What I do has nothing to do with you. I—"

"*Christ*. If you're leaving, I'm taking you and that's that."

"You have no right to—"

Carly broke off when he yanked her against him. Hard. It brought her up solidly against his chest and shut her up as probably nothing else would have. With the four-inch heels on her boots, it also brought her face almost level with his.

His jaw clenched, his nostrils flared slightly.

Carly swallowed as she looked at him. She was clamped hard along the length of his big body. He smelled fresh and male and musky. She'd never been this close to him before. Well, she had, but it had been over so fast she'd barely had time to appreciate the sensation and certainly not when he was looking at her with blazing eyes that dropped to her lips when she licked them. Not for the first time she mentally kicked herself for not taking advantage of that one time she'd had to touch him, to taste him, to just kid herself, even if it was for only a minute, that he was hers.

Carly didn't know what came over her, didn't know where she got the nerve, but she stood on tiptoes and put her mouth against his. In the instant she realized what she'd done, she pulled back, but he clamped a hand to the back of her head and held her in place, angled his head more to the side and…kissed her. *Deep.*

It could hardly be called a kiss. His tongue licked at her lips and then dipped inside and then out again in a rhythm that had her pressing her body farther into his to try to find some kind of relief from the fierce and immediate hunger raging through her. It felt as if he were fucking her with his mouth. It might have been brief, but her body remembered what he'd felt like inside her. She felt the clench between her legs, the moisture she couldn't prevent, the burn in the pit of her stomach, and felt so dizzy all she wanted to do was lie down. With him on top of her.

She felt his other hand against her lower back, pressing her into him and then she felt…*him.* He was huge and hard against her abdomen, even through two layers of denim.

Carly met his tongue with her own, groaning into his mouth, clutching at his shirt with fisted hands, trying to get even closer to him.

She heard the whistles and cheers as if from a distance, gradually permeating the fog of hunger and need clawing at her.

"About damn time." She heard someone call out as Rio pulled back.

He glanced around.

"*Fuck,*" he snarled. "Let's get out of here."

Carly shivered in the sharp, crisp air outside the bar and wrapped her arms around herself. She hated wearing anything that made her feel hot when she was out and never wanted the hassle of having to carry a jacket, which meant she usually froze going to and from.

Rio shrugged off his jacket and draped it across her shoulders. God, it smelled just like him, and with the warmth of his big body still lingering inside it, she could almost imagine it was his arms wrapped around her.

"Rio, no, you'll be cold. Take it back."

"You know me better than that."

Yeah, she did and that was half her problem. She knew him, needed him, *loved* him until she ached with it. He might be rough around the edges, but he had the ingrained manners of the most finely educated gentlemen. Compliments of a traditional father who believed women should be cared for and treasured, Rio had once told her.

The gesture, despite his anger and how much of a bitch she was being, brought the sting of tears to her eyes again and a thick knot to the back of her throat.

He walked beside her, his hands shoved into his pockets, his shoulders hunched against the cold. *Separate*. It just drove home how she'd become used to him walking beside her, close, holding her arm or his hand resting in the small of her back. She'd become used to his attentiveness, his consideration, his caring. And now? She only had herself to blame because he was already distancing himself from her and she couldn't help but push, and now she'd probably pushed him all the way out of her life.

Chapter Five

"Look, I'm sorry about the kiss, okay?"

"You are?"

She frowned. "You aren't?"

"I prefer to do my kissing without an audience."

What kind of answer was that?

She'd thought he'd just shrug it off. Since they'd come up to her apartment, the way he was looking at her was doing weird things to her stomach.

She wet her dry lips. Her breath caught with the realization that he'd been licking them not that long ago. She could almost imagine she could still taste him.

"Why did they say 'about time'? At the bar, I heard someone shout it."

"Cole. It was Cole and I guess I haven't been as subtle as I thought I had."

Huh?

His eyes were focused on her mouth. She held her breath as Rio walked to her and put a big hand on either side of her face, his fingers feeling a little rough against her cheeks. Her heart beat so hard she was sure he must be able to hear it.

"I'm done with subtle," he warned.

She swallowed. He looked at her for a second, two, before he lowered his mouth to hers. He kissed her in a string of nibbling forays, each one deeper than the last until his tongue was mating with hers in a series of movements that shot sensation straight between her legs, had her gasping for air, her hands fisted in his shirt on each side of his waist.

She registered his hands at the back of her neck but didn't realize his intention until she felt cool air against her naked breasts. She shivered in reaction.

He pulled back to look at her. Her breasts had to be completely bare to him, yet he didn't take his eyes from hers.

"I've never seen you naked before," he whispered, his voice guttural. "I've never touched you like this before, at least not with what's in my head right now…yet it doesn't feel as if I'm touching you for the first time, as if this is a first time for us. Do you know what I mean?"

Yeah, she knew exactly what he meant.

"I…" She moistened her lips, tasting him, and swallowed against the dryness of her throat. God, should she? "Um…technically, it's not…our first time, I mean."

The corner of his mouth lifted slightly, the look in his eyes searing.

"Doesn't count. I thought I was dreaming, for one."

The way he looked at her made her stomach flip-flop and she felt it low down in her abdomen. "You—you remember?"

"You thought I didn't?"

"You didn't say anything."

"Neither did you."

"Then how do you know it was real?"

"I did think it must have been all in my head until…"

"Until?"

"Until you cleaned me off. I knew it wasn't a dream for sure when you cleaned me off. No one else would have touched me so carefully, taking care of me like that. Carls…" He took a deep breath. "God, Carls, I didn't force you, did I?"

"Force me?"

"I outweigh you by probably a hundred pounds. I was…out of it, delirious at best. At first, anyway. If you'd wanted to, I'm not sure you could have stopped me and I—"

"I didn't even try."

He closed his eyes briefly. "Did you come?"

"You mean, you don't know?"

Rio shook his head.

"You asked me, you know. After…you asked me."

"And?"

"And…yeah, I did."

He let out a breath he must have been holding. His eyes finally lowered and he looked his fill, his gaze blazing a heat she could almost feel against her skin.

"I can do a lot better than that. In case you were wondering."

It had eaten at him, tormented him as nothing ever had, the thought he might have forced something on her she wouldn't have chosen otherwise. That and the probability she hadn't gotten any pleasure from it.

God, she was gorgeous. Her breasts were rounded, full on the bottom with small pink nipples on top. As much as he wanted to touch her, kiss her, lick and suck on them until she squirmed against him, there was something he wanted more, something he hadn't been able to get out of his head time and again as she'd tortured him in those barely there shorts.

"Turn around."

His voice came out rougher than he'd intended, but the punch to his gut he got almost brought him to his knees when she did as he asked without question.

He stepped to her back, his lips at her ear, the sweet scent of her making him lightheaded.

"I want to touch every inch of you. Hell, I want to *lick* every inch of you," he rasped.

His balls tightened when he felt the shiver chase across her skin. He ran his hands over her shoulders and down her bare back, trying to keep the touch light, around the slight indentation of her waist exposed by the low-slung jeans and up her front until both hands covered her breasts. He groaned as he weighed them, sliding his palms back and forth across her silky skin. He could feel the hard points of her nipples against their center and the short, erratic breaths she took each time he brushed against the sensitive peaks.

He bit her neck carefully. God, her skin was so soft and smooth right where it met her shoulder and she smelled so damn good.

Shaking with need, he eased one hand down the smooth skin of her abdomen and into the waistband of her jeans. He wasn't in the mood to drag it out as he once might have. His fingers delved straight under the thin panties and met hot, wet flesh. He smiled savagely when she jerked at the contact and was rewarded with a moan that sounded as if it were torn from her.

He glanced at her. Her head was thrown back against his shoulder, her eyes closed and her mouth slightly open as she panted.

He felt the pre-cum he couldn't have prevented if his life depended on it. It was almost as if his cock knew what he cupped in his palm…and it wanted. *He* wanted. God, he wanted nothing more than to yank down her jeans, bend her over and plow into her from behind until he was buried inside her as far as he could go. But first, first he wanted to explore the curve of her ass where it met her leg. The thought of it had driven him crazy for months when she'd pranced around in her miniscule shorts.

Carly couldn't prevent the whimper when he eased his hand from between her legs. The light touch hadn't been nearly enough. The protest she'd had ready died in her throat as he yanked at the button of her jeans, taking the zipper down in the same savage movement, and pushed the snug denim down her hips in rough, jerky tugs.

"You've got to be kidding me," he groaned.

"What?"

"You were wearing a thong almost the same as this the day we met."

All she could hear was the sound of her own breathing as he knelt on the floor behind her and cupped her bare buttocks exposed by the thong in his big, rough hands.

"And you would know that…how?"

"I saw the edge of your panties when you bent over. They were a blue-green color, edged with pink lace. I've never been able to get that sight out of my head."

Carly jumped when he put his mouth to her, opened it against her skin, low where her buttock met her thigh, and sucked lightly. She tried to drag in a much-needed breath when he continued to nibble, lick and suck on her, alternating back and forth between the cheeks of her ass until it felt as if he'd kissed every exposed inch of her.

"I can smell how wet you must be."

She gasped when he placed a hand against her lower back.

"Bend over."

Trembling, Carly grabbed for the nearest solid surface and ended up grasping one of her breakfast stools as she leaned forward.

"*Oh Christ,*" he breathed as he slid a single finger between her buttocks under the thin line of her thong and pulled it to the side. He rubbed lightly between her legs, up and down her slit, spreading her moisture until she couldn't keep her lower body still against the sensation. She just wanted to thrust back on his finger, impale herself on it, anything to stem the ache he'd created.

"Rio…"

"I want to learn every single thing you like. I want to know what turns you on, what makes you come. And then I'm going to start all over again."

Carly felt his hot breath against the throbbing wet flesh, felt him gently part her with his hands before he put his mouth to her and licked in a bold, firm stroke along the length of her, from the front as far as his tongue would reach all the way back to the puckered entrance of her ass. She gasped at the feel of the slight rasp of his whiskers against the sensitive flesh of her inner thighs. He repeated it, his wicked tongue licking at her, over and over, until she was struggling to breathe. She closed her eyes against the crescendo of need, but it only focused her senses on the soft, wet suckling sounds as he ate at her.

The ache between her legs, centered in her swollen clit, was so intense she stung from it. Carly reached between her legs, aching, desperate, the sensations almost more than she could stand. She just needed a firm touch, just one, but Rio grasped her hand before she could make contact with herself.

"No. As hot as that is, you'll get your pleasure from *my* mouth, *my* hands, *my* body. Maybe next time you can tease me with how and where you like to touch yourself. This time it's going to be all me."

"*Rio*… Rio, please…the bed."

"Not yet," he growled against her as he put his mouth to her again.

And then she felt the much-needed pressure against her clit…a finger, a thumb, rubbing in a circular motion in perfect concert to his relentless tongue, and just like that she was catapulted over.

Carly threw her head back as the sensations exploded between her legs and speared out in tingling rivulets to every part of her body. She called out, she must have, because her throat was dry or perhaps that was just because of the lungfuls of air she struggled to drag in.

She'd never come standing up before. Her legs still felt shaky, her breathing nowhere near normal when he dropped her on her bed. He must have carried her and he had to have been holding her up at the end, because she doubted she'd been able to stand through that on her own.

She watched, dazed, as he yanked her boots off, tugged her jeans down and flung the top that had gotten trapped around her hips aside.

When she tried to help him by lifting her hips up to take off her thong, he stopped her.

"No," he rasped. "Leave them on for a while longer."

Rio could still taste her against his tongue. The smell of her filled his nostrils as he took a deep breath. It was rich and musky and caused his cock to throb in response. He was already harder than he'd ever been before and now it was almost painful in its intensity.

There was the overwhelming need again. The screaming need to hurry, to take, to just…*fuck*. Mindlessly. He shook his head. He'd be damned if he'd jump her like a horny teen again. No, he was going to use every ounce of experience and expertise he'd ever gained. He was going to make her scream and beg and cry out his name. He was going to make her want him as she'd never wanted another man before and damn it, she wouldn't forget it or him anytime soon.

When her thighs shifted on the bed and his focus went between her legs, he knew he wanted to go down on her again. This time he wanted her completely open to him, her thighs up on his shoulders and her hands clutching his hair, showing him just how she wanted it. And he wanted to look up at her and watch her face when she went over.

He nudged her thighs a little farther apart as he settled between her legs on the bed. He kissed and licked the smooth skin on the inside of her knee and worked his way up with a string of kisses until he met the edge of her panties. She smelled incredible, her release making it richer, sweeter, *hotter*. He skipped to the other side and made his way up to her other knee. By the time he licked his way back down again she was writhing on the bed, panting, her hips pushing up to him.

"Don't you dare," she whispered, her voice ragged.

He laughed against her. He'd been going to skip across the triangle of silk again. Instead he relented, using two fingers to gently ease the soaked panel of her panties aside, and blew gently against her. She shivered and groaned. She was golden here too. Soft, short strands of light hair, trimmed into a neat strip above her wet, swollen folds. Beneath she was pink and glistening, her clit a small, engorged bud. He could barely wait to put his mouth to her again and lick up all of the juice he could see.

He put his middle finger to her, traced through her folds carefully and probed gently. He let out a breath when she flexed against him in invitation. She was hot and tight and he sank his finger in slowly until he could go no farther.

He swallowed in awe as he withdrew and sank back in, again and again, as slow as he could. Her eyes were closed now, her hips rocking back and forth as he fucked her with his finger, a small, carnal sound escaping her throat each time he went deep. He added a second finger. It was a snug fit, but he strummed her clit with the thumb of his other hand and was rewarded when she arched back and her hands fisted in the strands of his hair. She was thrusting in earnest now against his hand, pushing on his head, urging him down to her.

"I want to make you come with my mouth again," he warned.

She moaned. He put his mouth to her, sucked on her clit strongly and just like that he knew she went over. She cried out, thrusting her lower body against his lashing tongue in short, sharp movements. He used his free forearm across her abdomen to hold her still, to make sure he could keep his mouth against her until she finished.

Chapter Six

Carly unclenched her hands and threaded her fingers through the length of Rio's dark, silky hair as he made his way up her body, stopping to nibble on the underside of one breast. She stilled when she felt the rough tickle of the fabric of his jeans against her thigh.

Oh God. She'd come. *Twice.* And he still had all of his clothes on.

Carly pushed herself up with an effort. She'd never felt so weak, but there was determination in the jut of her jaw and strength in the hand she used to urge him over and onto his back.

His cheeks were flushed, his eyes dark with need. His breathing was ragged and she loved the way his gaze traced across her naked breasts as if he couldn't help himself.

"Undo my shirt."

His voice was low and rough and his insistence caused a jolt low in her abdomen that should have been pretty much impossible.

"Undo it," he urged. "I've imagined your hands on me so many times, taking my clothes off, touching me. Do it. *Please.*"

She'd touched him plenty of times before. She knew how hard he worked to stay in shape and how built he was. She still jolted as she laid her palms on his chest. He felt so hard. She could feel the raging heat from his big body through the smooth cotton of his shirt.

Carly slowly undid the buttons and pushed the fabric aside. She ran her hands lightly down his chest, his tight abdomen. How many times had she wished she had the right to touch him like this? To reach out whenever she wanted and put her hand on him and have her touch accepted, welcomed?

She saw him swallow and his jaw clench when her fingers dipped lightly into the waistband of his jeans. She jerked the buttons open awkwardly, wondering how she was going to get them down when he suddenly lifted his hips off the bed and yanked the jeans and his underwear down to the tops of his thighs, as if he couldn't wait any longer.

She'd meant to undress him with finesse, with a deliberate slowness, to torment him until he couldn't stand it, but she forgot all of that when she saw his beautiful cock.

"Oh, Rio."

It was long and thick, lying up against the flat plane of his abdomen. The fleeting view she'd had of him before had hardly done justice to a cock that was big and hard and so rigid she could see his heartbeat as it flexed.

She knelt between his legs, her throat dry at the spectacular view, his musky scent surrounding her, his arousal front and center in her line of sight.

He groaned at the first contact of her tongue, lifting off the bed and up onto his forearms as she licked up his length and gave a small sucking kiss on the head. His eyes were dark and dazed.

"Carls, I'm not going to be able stand this for long," he warned.

After what he'd done to her? Twice?

"Suck it up, big guy."

Suck. Rio swore he almost came just hearing her say the word, her lips looking wet from doing just that to him.

He spread his legs as far as the jeans would allow, to give her better access when she bent to him again.

"Go easy, okay?" he asked when she'd barely breathed on him.

He eased her back when she'd done no more than lick up his length a couple of times. He couldn't stand it and as much as he'd love to spill himself into her mouth or all over her beautiful breasts, he just wanted inside her. *Now.*

"Enough."

"Rio, *no*, I'm—"

"Yeah, you looked as if you were really getting into it, but I'm not going to be able to last as it is. We'll see how easily you can drive me out of my mind once the edge is taken off. Later."

He rolled to his feet beside the bed and flung his shirt off, pushed his jeans and underwear down and toed off his shoes, all the while his gaze traced the along the lines of her body as she turned around and sat back on the bed.

"But…"

"Later," he reassured her. "Trust me. *Later.*"

His heart thundered in his chest, his blood a roar in his ears as he looked at her. Every other woman he'd ever looked at, touched or been inside of faded from his mind. God, did she have any idea how fucking beautiful she was?

He crawled up and over her, trying to control the tremor he felt in his hand as he laid it on her smooth thigh and she eased back on the bed under him.

"You have no idea the things I want to do to you, how I want to do them to you."

He bent down and took a nipple between his lips, tonguing it against the roof of his mouth, celebrating the way she clutched at his shoulders and gasped when he laved the other nipple in the same way.

"Anything. However you want. *Please.*"

Her legs moved restlessly under him when he switched nipples again.

"Rio, *please*. Touch me," she begged when he didn't say anything. He had no doubt where she wanted him to touch her, but he needed a minute, a minute to get the red haze of lust under control so he didn't come the minute he got inside her.

"Touch yourself."

"Rio…"

"Touch yourself. Show me how you want me to make love to you."

Rio angled himself so he could see the hand she eased between her legs. His heart thundered even more. Instead of the teasing touches he'd braced himself for, she slid two fingers deep inside herself without hesitation and pumped her hand back and forth.

"Hard. And fast. I want it hard and fast," she panted.

Fuck.

Rio grasped her hand and pulled it from her body. The next time she came he was going to be inside her and it looked as if she'd been about to send herself over.

He eased his weight down on top of her, angled himself so that his cock was poised over her hot, wet opening and paused. Carly clutched at his shoulders, clasped her thighs around his tightly. Anticipation was a sizzle that ran through every nerve ending in his body as he looked down at her.

"*Rio*… Hurry up already."

Oh God, this was what all those other women had experienced. She'd known instinctively this is how he'd be in bed, playful, bold, uninhibited…and completely addictive.

"Carls. Look at me."

Carly lifted her eyes to his with an effort, her lids like lead. She inhaled sharply when she felt him sink more of his weight onto her, his body pressing more urgently against hers. His face was directly above hers, his forearms bracketing each side of her head. His eyes blazed with need, his jaw clenched tight with the effort it must have cost him to hold off pushing into her.

"I love you, you know that, right?" he rasped.

Everything inside her went still. Surely he didn't... Did he just say...what she thought he said? And even if he did? Carly tried to temper the flare of whatever it was that sprang to life at the words. There's no way he meant it like she wanted, needed, *ached* for him to mean it. He couldn't have. Could he?

"Rio." The sigh turned into a gasp as he drove into her in a single move that buried him all the way inside her.

"Carls, you're...we... *Christ*, it..."

She trembled as she looked up at him, feeling stretched and full, braced for another thrust that hadn't happened yet.

"Yeah..."

He brushed a strand of hair back from her forehead with a hand she swore shook.

"I thought I must have dreamed this part, at least," he ground out.

"This part?"

"Yeah, how incredible it feels. God, have I ever once told you how beautiful you are?" His voice was low, intense.

"No..."

"Then you should probably kick my ass."

"I have better things to do with your ass right now. Like—*move it*."

Carly groaned when he began thrusting in a steady, deep rhythm. He clasped her hands in his and raised them up above her head, holding her stretched out beneath him. She couldn't use them for leverage. There was nothing she could do but meet his thrusts with her own lower body movements, making a perfect counter to his as best she could. This was Rio and he was merely holding her, yet it fired off every fantasy she'd ever had about being dominated, except this was much more exciting then anything else she'd ever experienced or fantasized about before.

Rio bent and licked her nipple with firm laps of his tongue in the same maddening rhythm as his body into hers.

"Guess…I now know…what all the…screaming's about," she gasped between thrusts. "Why haven't we…ever done this before now?"

"Because I'm an idiot."

Carly closed her eyes against the sensations as his thrusts became faster, harder. Every time he thrust in, he flexed his hips too so that his body hair ground against her clit. Tremors pulsed and rolled outward through her body from the contact. He was rocketing her to another release that gave her a moment's panic before she stiffened, the ecstasy almost painful as she was thrown headfirst into a series of waves so intense they racked her body with heaving shudders.

She was vaguely away of Rio's shout, his face buried against her neck as he groaned deeply, his body jerking against her in what seemed to be an endless sequence of spasms to match her own.

* * * * *

"We didn't use anything. *Again.*"

Carly was trying her damnedest to get her breathing under control. It wasn't easy when he was still buried deep inside her and she could feel the thunder of his heart against her chest.

"I—it's okay."

Rio fingered a strip of her hair, rubbing the strands gently. "I've never done it without a rubber before, not even when I was little more than a kid, more horny than smart."

"Me either."

"Even with what's his name?"

It struck Carly that Rio had never actually used Greg's name whenever he referred to him.

"Yeah, even with him."

Rio frowned. "Did he—"

"Do you really want to talk about Greg right now?"

"*No*. No. Um…what about—"

"I'm on the Pill."

Rio eased back from her, withdrawing from her body carefully. She couldn't prevent the small gasp when he finally slid free.

God, he was building up to something.

Carly steeled herself for it, but all of a sudden she just couldn't wait.

"Damn it, Rio. If you tell me you're sorry…"

Carly stopped when her throat threatened to close completely. She wouldn't break down in front of him. She wouldn't.

He touched a fingertip to her bottom lip.

"Carly, do you have any idea how much I wanted to kiss you that day in the elevator, back you up against the wall and just go for it? My reaction to you was not one I should have had. I had a girlfriend and we… I thought… *Christ*, one look at you and I knew the feelings I had for Liz were lukewarm at best compared to what I was feeling for you. I didn't know you, I hadn't touched you and I might never get the chance, but I knew right then it was over with Liz. It had to be."

"You broke up with Liz because of *me*?"

"No. I broke up with Liz because I shouldn't have gotten a hard-on for another woman when I was with her. I didn't want to hurt her, but I dragged it out, probably made it worse. It took three months, all the while I tried to keep away from you, but by then you were dating pretty hard core. So, I cooled my heels."

Yeah, she remembered. The girlfriend pact. They'd made a pact to accept dates from any and all guys who asked. For six months. No exceptions. Supposedly to find "Mr. Right". What a disaster it'd been.

"By the time I thought the timing was right, you were hot and heavy with..."

"Greg."

"Yeah. I figured it'd run its course and I'd be ready. In the meantime we were hanging out, became friends...and I just..."

"I felt it too, you know. That day in the elevator. God, Rio, do you know what it's been like for me?" Carly whispered. "Watching you with other women, watching them hit on you, watching you smile at them, touch them, God, even hearing you *fuck* them? I told myself I never had a chance, that if you'd been interested I would have known, you would have shown me, but it didn't stop the pain each and every time you hooked up with someone."

His jaw clenched and his eyes bore into hers. The satisfaction that had been etched into his features was gone in an instant. "I know every time you've been out with a guy or had someone over at your place. I know every time a guy's spent the night here and I know every night you never came home. *Every. Single. Fucking. Time.* So, yeah, I think I've got a clue."

Carly blinked. She'd heard more swear words from him lately than from the entire time she'd known him. The emotional edge to his voice was one she'd never heard before and it cut into her.

"You make it sound as if it's been a lot. It—"

"It wouldn't have mattered how many. One guy, one time, was too many."

"Rio—"

"Carls, look... I don't want to think about you with other guys, okay? You're beautiful, gorgeous. I'd be an idiot to have a problem with the fact that there've been others. But I don't... I don't want to think about it. I just want to think about how it was with us."

Carly swallowed. "Okay."

He pushed a strand of hair back from her forehead. "It blew my mind, you know."

Her heartbeat kicked up a notch. "Yeah?"

"Oh yeah."

"So, you…you want to be a…friend with benefits, Rio? Is that it?"

"No!"

Carly couldn't help the flinch.

"No," he repeated, his voice quieter but firm. "I don't want any sort of arrangement like that. Where we sleep together when neither of us is seeing anyone else or even if we are? God, *no*."

"Then what? You need to give me some clue here, because—"

"Didn't you hear what I told you before?"

Her stomach lurched. "That was…"

In the heat of the moment.

Rio cupped her jaw and lowered his mouth to hers, sinking into a kiss that had intimacy and familiarity written all over it. The heat of his big body seared hers, scorching between her legs when his tongue moved urgently against hers. By the time he pulled back she was clutching his shoulders, her lips clinging to his, her breathing unsteady.

"And if that doesn't tell you anything," he groaned, "I'll say it again, say what my body's already told you. I love you, Carly. Not as a friend, but as a man loves his woman. I'd kill to protect you, I'd give my life for yours, I'd—"

Carly put a finger to his lips shakily. *Oh God*. Every part of her felt as if it were trembling, trembling in reaction, in wonder, in awe. "Okay, I think I get the message."

He sucked the tip into his mouth. It should have been impossible, but pure heat and moisture bloomed between her legs again.

"You're not going to ask me how *I* feel?" she breathed.

He bit and then kissed the thick pad of her hand. His smile was full of male confidence. "You wouldn't have let me do the things I did to you if you didn't have feelings for me and you wouldn't have given yourself to me the way you did if you didn't love me."

Cocky. That's what he was, but dead right. She'd tell him so the next time she had him in her mouth.

"So, where do we go from here?"

His smile broadened. It was sinful and wicked and caused her stomach to lurch in response. He ran his hand down the slope of her body to rest over the slight curve of her abdomen, his hand splayed wide. There was no doubt it was a touch of possession. His gaze swept over her features before locking on hers.

"You pay up."

"Pay up?"

"Yeah, you remember the bet. You owe me."

"You…you want to talk about…that stupid bet?"

"Nope. I want you to pay up. I won."

Carly swallowed, his touch making it difficult to focus. She moved her legs, barely able to keep still and gasped when she brushed up against the hair-roughened lengths of his. "How do you figure?"

"I…ah, the Pink Pony. I might have had a call there a few weeks back."

She was becoming used to that smug smile and it did things to her insides she could become addicted to. The sheepishness was new. "A call?"

He smiled. "Yeah. Some old guy collapsed. Heart attack. I think the lap dance he might have been having at the time was too much for him."

Carly just looked at him as it dawned on her. He'd known he'd already won when he made that outrageous bet.

"And no one on staff was called Honey," he added.

She frowned. "Oh? And you know that how?"

He laughed and smoothed the lines between her eyes with his thumb. "They all seemed very nice, very grateful the old guy was going to be okay. Introduced themselves to me and the guys."

Carly couldn't prevent the pang at the picture she got. It was sharp, intense. Rio surrounded by beautiful, half-naked women, all vying for his attention.

"Yeah, I'll bet."

He laughed again and then sobered, running the pad of his thumb across her lower lip, his gaze focused on her mouth. "I couldn't describe a single one of them if my life depended on it, but I know there wasn't a Honey among them, baby."

Carly took a deep breath at the look in his eyes, the term she should have had an issue with but somehow didn't, and tried not to squirm.

"And what are you claiming as your favor?"

He felt the tremor that ran through her body.

"Don't be scared. I wouldn't ever hurt you. I'd cut off my own arm first."

"I'm not scared. God, Rio don't you know I'd let you do anything you wanted to me? I'm just…I mean, I… I wouldn't want to disappoint you."

Rio couldn't help the flare of triumph that roared through him or the sudden, aching hardness of his body that should have been impossible, at least so soon.

"Are you kidding? Do you realize how we fit, how we are together? God, it's as if you were made just for me. I'd give you whatever you wanted, do whatever you needed. I'll only ever want to please you, but make no mistake—I want to do every hot, sexy, dirty thing I've ever thought about to you, *with* you. But my prize?"

He watched as she licked her lips and looked at him. He saw it, the trust, the acceptance and the need. The surge of lust and love that slammed into him would have knocked him on his ass if he hadn't already been lying down. He'd thought hard about what he'd collect when the time came—hell, he'd tormented himself with it. *And now*? Now everything was different.

He took a deep breath. "I want you to be mine. I want to know I'm the only man you'll let touch you, who'll ever see you like this, the only one you want. I want it to be the 'there's no doubt every other guy knows you belong to me' kind of mine. I want *you*, Carls. Just you."

Rio couldn't prevent the clench in his gut at the look in her eyes when she raised a soft hand to his cheek. It was sultry and sexy as hell and it was all for him.

"On one condition," she whispered.

"Yeah?"

"That I get my turn to drive you out of your mind. That I get to do more than just lick you a couple of times. And that I get to start *right now*."

PLAY ME

Dedication

To all those who "pay it forward" in this industry. Your support, encouragement and generosity are much appreciated. I wanna be like you when I grow up!

Trademarks Acknowledgement

The author acknowledges the trademarked status and trademark owners of the following wordmarks mentioned in this work of fiction:

Mercedes: DaimlerChrysler AG Corporation

Styrofoam: Dow Chemical Company

Chapter One

Crap.

Lily didn't need a lot of brains to know this was not a good area. In fact, if the barbed wire across everything and bars on every visible window were anything to go on it was bad—and her car had just broken down right in the middle of it. Well, okay it wasn't exactly *her* car, but at the moment all that mattered was that the damn thing wouldn't go.

She took a deep breath, the cold lump of dread heavy in her stomach. It spread through her limbs in numbing waves and she shivered, even though it wasn't that cold inside the car.

Oh God, she should've known better.

She'd lived in LA long enough to know what happened to unsuspecting tourists when they got off a freeway at the wrong exit or turned down the wrong street. But who could blame her? The image of her fiancé, pants down around his ankles while he...*screwed* some bimbo up against the bathroom counter had been burned into her brain.

Stupid. She'd been so stupid.

Lily rested her forehead against the steering wheel and closed her eyes. She'd deal with all that later because right now she had a bigger problem. Despite how she'd begged and how much she'd offered, none of the cab companies she'd called would come pick her up.

Crap. It had to be really, *really* bad.

"Yeah?"

The rough voice made her jump, almost dropping her phone. She'd already dialed the number five times—

incessantly, *desperately*—without an answer. Really, why would this time be any different?

"Um...hello." She lifted her head, cleared her throat and took a deep breath to calm her churning stomach. "My car's broken down and—"

"Look, lady, I'm just about to close it down for the night, so—"

"*Wait*, please, I—I'm running out of options here." The woman at the last cab company had finally given her this number and wished her luck before hanging up. She knew she sounded frantic, but... "No one else will come and—"

"Where are you?"

Lily rattled off the location according to the map on her phone and held her breath. Sure enough, there was the pause. Every other call had ended right about now.

"What kind of car is it?"

What kind of— Did that really matter?

"Ah, it's a...Mercedes. Um— Does McLaren something or other mean anything to—"

"*Fuck.*"

The curse was savage, but there was an underlying edge of something that caused her feeling of dread to turn into sharp, ice-cold fear.

She licked her lips. "I—"

"Are you alone?"

"Y-Yes."

"Are you in the vehicle?"

She frowned. "Yes, I—"

"You need to get out of the car. *Now.*"

Was he insane?

Lily looked around. It was dark. Many of the street lights were either broken or missing altogether. The empty windows of the surrounding dilapidated buildings looked sinister in the dim lighting. God, everything looked sinister.

"What's your name?" he asked when she didn't say anything.

"Lily. Lily Hamilton, but—"

"Look, Lily…I want you to listen to me and listen very carefully, okay?"

She heard the urgency balanced with deliberate calm in his deep voice and everything in her went still.

"Okay," she whispered carefully.

"You need to find someplace to hide. *Outside* the car."

"Hide? But—"

"Close enough that you can still see it."

Her eyes scanned the side of the road. "There's some bushes, but—"

"You'll be completely hidden?"

"I…I think so."

"Go there. *Right now.*"

"But—"

"Lily, you can't stay in the car. I know it feels counterintuitive, but you're not safe sitting in a locked car, especially a car worth half a million bucks. It's a fucking beacon. Do you understand?"

Lily's heart leapt. She'd known Ian had paid a fortune for the car, but really?

"They can't get to you if they don't know you're there," he added quietly.

"They?"

"I don't know how much longer you've got, but someone's going to come along. Someone you won't want to meet, trust me. Do you understand what I'm saying?"

When she didn't respond, he swore again. *"Lily—"*

"All right," she relented in a shaky whisper.

"Keep away from any light. Stay completely out of sight. Make yourself as small as possible and put your phone on silent. *Go.*"

"Who are you?" she whispered into the thick silence as she got out of the car and closed the door. She grasped the long skirt of her dress in one shaking hand and carefully picked her way across the cracked, uneven pavement. She stepped into damp soil, thick weeds and crouched down behind a squat bush. Yep, the expensive stilettos she hadn't wanted to buy in the first place were now officially ruined.

"I'm…Gabe. I'll be there as soon as I can, but I'm at least thirty minutes out. Regardless of what happens, what you may see or hear—stay put. Got it?"

Lily swallowed and nodded, knowing he couldn't see it, but unable to get an answer past the clench of her throat. She dropped her forehead onto her knees.

"Gabe?" she whispered instead, her voice barely audible, her hand aching from holding the phone so tight.

"Yeah?"

"I— Thank you."

He was silent for several seconds. "Don't thank me yet. I have to get to you first. Just don't move."

Lily shivered. "Hurry, okay? Please just…hurry."

* * * * *

"Fuck, man. Do you know what the *fuck* this *is*?"

Oh God, she'd had only minutes.

Lily didn't have to know anything about gangs or street violence. She didn't need to be able to recite the shocking crime statistics. All she knew was if she'd stayed in the car… Well, the possibilities were seriously scary.

She hadn't been able to stop the trembling that racked her entire body since the dark, ominous car had pulled to an almost-silent stop—right next to the car she'd been sitting in. It was partly from the cold and damp, partly from the cramped way she was sitting, but mostly from sheer and utter terror.

There were four of them—circling the car like vultures, their gazes cold and dead, their every movement aggressive, menacing. Their language was explicit and brutal, an overlay to the violence she sensed simmering between them as they fought over what to do with the car. They reminded her of the most dangerous of predators where one false move could incite a mindless frenzy.

She tried to slow her breathing, her heart beating so fast she was afraid they'd be able to hear it. Her eyes tightly closed, she pressed her forehead down onto her knees and rocked herself with a slight motion she hoped would somehow keep hysteria from taking over completely. It was futile, she knew it was, but she tried to will herself invisible, convince herself it was all a bad dream and wish she was anywhere but here. The acrid taste and smell of her own fear told her it was only too real and she'd be forced to live through it, to endure it. She could only hope to survive—whatever it was.

Oh God, where was he?

As soon as she thought of Gabe, a wave of panic swept through her. What would happen when he turned up and was confronted by these guys? What could he possibly do against them anyway? Was he even coming?

She started as another vehicle pulled to a stop in a loud screech, the roar of the engine deep and powerful, and squeezed her eyes more tightly closed. She put her hand over her mouth at the soft sound she couldn't prevent.

"Fuck off, man. We were here first."

Oh God, it was a convention for bad guys. Or maybe she'd be witness to a war? Well, she could only hope they all killed each other. Steeling herself, she lifted her head slowly and then froze.

She didn't know why or how, but she knew without a doubt it was *him*. Gabe.

He stood by a huge tow truck parked at an angle to the car, its engine still running, the driver's door standing wide open. He wore a beat-up, old leather jacket and worn jeans. His legs were spread in what looked to be a relaxed stance, but there was an air of coiled readiness in every line of his big, powerful body. Heck, his stance literally screamed "don't mess with me". He took in the scene in a single, sweeping glance.

"Why don't you boys get lost?"

Lily's heart leapt. That voice. It was the same, yet vibrated with a quiet menace and a confidence that had the predators all stilling.

One of them made a step toward him and she gasped behind her fingers. Gabe had pulled a gun in a flash, not pointing it at the one who'd moved, but at the one Lily had assumed was the leader of sorts. He hadn't had a chance to observe and hear them the way she had, so how had he known? They all froze.

The guy slowly lifted a hand to the others. "Hey, man...it's cool, we're cool, we can—"

"Lily? Lily, it's Gabe."

He glanced right at her for a split second as if she were in clear sight. She'd probably deluded herself into thinking they couldn't see her, that they wouldn't find her. It'd probably just been a matter of time.

"Lily? Move it. *Now.*"

Lily uncurled her legs and stumbled when she tried to stand. She'd sat in the cramped position for so long, her legs were stiff. And she was shaking. *Hard.* She'd been shaking since she'd gotten out of the car, deep inside her bones, and hadn't been able to make it stop.

She staggered from behind the bush, almost falling in the ridiculous heels. Her mouth was so dry, she could barely swallow. She'd never felt so self-conscious, so aware of her own vulnerabilities, so much like *prey* as she became the focus of four sets of coldly assessing eyes and several low murmurs she was glad she couldn't make out. The sleek, floor-length, slip-style dress had seemed the perfect outfit for the party. Now all she could think about was how closely the thin silk skimmed the lines of her body. It felt as if each and every one of them could see right through it.

Gabe hadn't taken his eyes off the group, but she felt his gaze nevertheless. She focused on him, on putting one foot in front of the other, trying to block out the hungry gazes she could almost feel. She fought the urge to run to him, press her chilled-to-the-core body to his and burrow into him. For warmth, for protection, for…comfort.

He glanced at her briefly when she reached him and she shivered anew at the all-encompassing look in his dark, hooded eyes. There was no explicit speculation, no hard-edged assessment, but she felt the look as if it were a physical touch all the way to her toes.

Lily gasped when one of the other men made a slight movement and Gabe's other hand came up so quickly, it was a blur. He'd pulled a second gun from somewhere. Standing with his feet spread, a gun in each hand, he looked as tough and as hard as they did and a frisson of alarm ran through her.

"I just want the woman," he ground out. "You want to make it personal, go ahead." It was a warning that couldn't be mistaken for anything but a deadly promise.

He jerked his head toward the truck. "Get in."

Gabe threw himself into the cab, shoving the woman across to the passenger side with the bulk of his body and had the truck moving before he'd jerked the door closed.

"What about the car?"

Gabe threw her an incredulous look. *Was she fucking kidding?* They'd probably just escaped with their lives and—

He cringed at the loud popping noise.

"What was that?" she gasped.

"Gunshot." Gabe glanced in the rearview mirror. "Didn't hit anything vital."

He hoped.

"Are you…going to shoot back?"

His raised one eyebrow as he glanced at her again quickly. She was pushing long, soft-looking strands of hair off her face and trying to find the seat belt. He felt his mouth twitch. "No."

Lily. The name suited her. She was pale and elegant, beautiful in a delicate, refined way. Jeez, she looked like some kind of fucking princess, with her floor-length, silver dress, the glittery little bag and fancy shoes. And he'd bet the rocks she was wearing were the real deal. She looked expensively pampered and smelled *rich.* It was subtle, but the scent filled the stale air of the truck and made him feel almost lightheaded.

She wouldn't have lasted an hour with those thugs and his dumb-ass protective instincts fired again. Where the hell did it ever get him except in a shitload of trouble and a world of hurt? Anyone just had to look at his face to know what had happened the last time he'd tried to help a woman. He flexed his shoulders and felt the tenderness all the way down each side. Yeah, he'd probably been lucky to only end up with a cracked rib and a few bruises.

She was staring at him. Her face looked white against the paleness of her hair. He glanced down at her hands clasped together in her lap. Even though her knuckles were white with how hard she was clenching them, he still noticed their shaking.

"Here."

He handed her the half-empty coffee sitting in his console. It was probably warm, but barely. She wrapped her hands around the large Styrofoam cup and took several big mouthfuls.

Gabe drew a deep breath and let it out when he entered the freeway. No one was following. And why would they? They had a hell of a find to keep them busy.

He wanted to ask her what the *hell* she thought she was doing driving around—alone—at 2:00 in the morning, but what business was it of his? Besides, he had enough complications of his own. He cast another quick glance in her direction.

"You okay?"

She nodded.

"You don't look the type to steal a car."

Her head came up quickly. "Steal?"

"Yeah, the wheels you were driving. It was reported stolen an hour or so ago."

She looked at him blankly for one beat, two, glanced down at his scanner and then turned to look out the window. "Men are jerks."

"Yeah, pretty much." Gabe turned his attention back to the road. "Some of us are just better at it than others."

"Well, my fiancé could give lessons," she muttered.

"Fiancé?"

She belonged to someone. Of course she did. Fuck, just look at her. The once-fancy hairdo, the jewelry and that dress...if you could call it a dress. It looked like what he imagined rich chicks wore to sleep in. He already knew she didn't have a bra on, but she was either wearing a barely there thong or nothing at all under it. As he'd jumped in behind her and grasped her hips to shove her across the seat, the silky fabric had hugged the curves of her body and rode right up between the cheeks of her ass. *Jesus.* Not a single panty line in sight. He'd had other things to worry about at the time, but...he'd still looked. Hard.

Lily stared down at the rock on her finger. It was gaudy and cold, too large for her slender hand and fingers, but Ian hadn't cared about any of that. She'd barely contained her disappointment when he'd given it to her. She'd hungered for him to understand enough about her to give her something she really wanted, something that was *her*, something she totally loved. Instead he'd bought a ring that projected more about him and she'd hated it. But she'd let it go. Just like everything else, she'd been the one to bend. Dammit, she'd tried so hard and he'd been… The thing of it was, it probably hadn't been the first time. There'd been enough clues. She'd just been too stupid, too gullible and too willing to settle, to actually pay attention.

"Not anymore."

She tugged the ring off roughly and flicked it through the open window before she thought better of it.

Gabe whistled and glanced in the rearview mirror. "Ah…you sure you want to do that? It looked…expensive. I could probably pinpoint where it went if you want it back."

"No."

She never wanted to see *it* or Ian again.

Although he hadn't moved or said anything, she'd been aware the instant Gabe had relaxed. She'd sensed an uncoiling of rigidly held muscles and a relaxation of a focus so intense it made her want to squirm every time he looked at her. Maybe it was because he was just so rough and rugged, hardened in a way she'd never gone for before. Or maybe it was because he was just so…big. And he looked as if he'd been in a fight recently. There was bruising around one of his eyes and a scrape on his cheek and jaw as if he'd been dragged across rough asphalt on his face, and not too long ago. With his dark hair and dark eyes, he carried a dangerous air about him that should've scared her, but the tingle of awareness she felt wasn't fear. No, now she knew what real fear was, what it felt like, what it tasted like. Besides, she should be glad he was the bad guy type, otherwise… She shivered. She didn't want to think about what could have happened, what almost did happen.

She cleared her throat. "Shouldn't you—*we*—call the police?"

The corner of his mouth kicked up again.

Had she said something funny?

"They'll be long gone. So will the car."

"But they shot at us."

He shrugged.

Lily swallowed. God, all of this seemed too ordinary for him. What kind of tow truck driver carried a gun—make that two guns—thought nothing of going face-to-face with a street gang and shrugged at being shot at? Not that she'd known many tow truck drivers, of course. Actually, make that any.

One of the guns was tucked into the waistband of his jeans. It looked snug against his flat stomach and stood out dark and lethal against the white of his t-shirt. When her gaze skirted the large bulge between his legs, she licked her dry lips.

"You're not worried you're going to shoot your…er…"

He glanced at her quickly. This time it was a half-smile showing a flash of very white, even teeth when he saw where she was looking.

"Safety's on."

God, she'd never even seen a real gun before, had never known anyone who actually owned one, and he was just so nonchalant about it. About all of it.

"A-Are you supposed to have that? I mean…is it legal?"

Again with the mouth quirk. "Yeah, it's legal." He turned his attention back to the road. "Where can I take you, Lily?"

He was all business again. The smile and spark she'd glimpsed briefly completely gone. Her name sounded odd in his deep, rough voice though. There was an intimacy to it that shouldn't have been there. Or maybe she was just delusional. She was entitled to some delusion, right?

"Home. I just want to go home."

Chapter Two

"Um…do I owe you anything?"

Gabe clenched his jaw and tried not to let his dirty fucking mind go there. "No."

"Maybe you'd like to…come in?"

He looked up at the three-story house he'd parked in front of. A half-block from the waves in Hermosa Beach, it must be worth a small fortune. Probably rocked some awesome views of the Pacific and couldn't have been more different from the four walls where he currently crashed and slept. Or tried to.

"For what?"

He knew he was being an asshole. He'd noticed her interest. It would have been hard to miss. The way she'd been looking at him was enough to have his blood boiling and him wondering if her dress was as silky as it looked sliding across her smooth skin. Yeah, as he yanked it up and checked for himself if she was wearing any panties. Where the *fuck* she did get off looking at him like that, anyway? She'd probably narrowly escaped being raped, possibly beaten, maybe even killed. Besides, she didn't look the type to go for sex of the one-night stand variety. He was too revved up to be slow and tender and he didn't think she went for sex of the rough variety either. And that was all he had in him now anyway.

Before she could answer he swung out of the truck and slammed the door, harder than he needed to. She already had hers open, sitting sideways and trying to figure out how to get down when he got around to her side. He'd pegged her for the type to expect guys to open doors for her. Or maybe she just didn't expect it of someone like him and that just pissed him off.

As she glanced up at him in surprise, he got a punch to his gut that had nothing to do with the fact the thin strap of her dress had slipped down one arm, exposing the top of a creamy breast—although that in itself was pretty fucking amazing—and everything to do with her eyes. It was the first time he'd gotten a good look at them. They were green—a clear, bright green and her gaze was… *Christ,* totally wide open to him.

He reached out, grasped her upper arms and lifted her from the truck. He got a quick impression of soft, smooth skin before he let her go. It was all he allowed himself. He slammed her door as well. The shot of sound perfectly suited his mood.

"How about…um, some more coffee? Would you—"

"Good night, Lily." He took one long, last look at her before he turned away.

"Wait." She put a hand on his forearm.

Even though he couldn't feel her touch through the thick leather, just the thought of it caused his body to heat, tighten.

"I wanted to thank you for—"

He raked her head to foot with a look he couldn't help. "By offering to let me fuck you?"

"What?" she gasped. Her hand dropped. "No, I—"

"A 'thanks' would have been sufficient."

"You—"

In the blink of an eye, he'd backed her up against the truck and pressed into her, trapping her between the smooth metal and the hard length of his body. God, she was so damn soft. Before he thought better of it, he lowered his head and molded his lips to hers. He didn't even give her a chance to react before he ran his tongue boldly over her lips and between them. He cursed at the shaft of heat that arrowed down right into his cock and tightened his balls.

He dipped inside her mouth once, twice, a third time before he pulled sharply back. It had felt too much as if he were fucking her mouth with his tongue. He took a deep breath in a futile effort to stem the rapid thud of his heart and fought the urge to thrust his hips against her, to use his thigh to nudge her legs apart so he could rub himself against her heat. God, he was so hard—rock hard—she had to be able to feel it through his jeans and the barely there dress.

Dammit.

That's not what he'd intended. At least not the getting hard part.

Her lips were wet and swollen, her breathing quick and her eyes wide. Yeah, he'd probably shocked and scared the hell out of her with that move.

Good.

"Hard, fast and rough," he grated. "That's how I like it, that's what I have in me. You don't want any part of that. Trust me."

She finally had some color on her cheeks and it looked good on her. Too fucking good. He began to swing away from her, resolved to the fact he'd never see her again when she laid both her hands flat on his chest. He froze. She'd put them inside his jacket against his t-shirt and damn if he couldn't feel the heat of her through it.

Christ, but she smelled sweet.

He felt the tremble, saw her swallow, yet she still reached up and pressed her mouth against his. He could have pulled back in time or moved away—but he didn't. And then he couldn't. After everything he'd seen and done, Gabe would have bet his life nothing could surprise him anymore. He was dead wrong.

She nibbled along his bottom lip, used her tongue to taste the shape of his mouth. It wasn't practiced. In fact, it was a whole lot of clumsy. And a hell of a turn-on. The soft, tentative movements caused a curl in his gut he hadn't experienced in a long time.

He felt her soft breath fan out against his mouth as she pulled back and that sigh was his undoing. Before he had time to think about it, he grasped the back of her head with a hand he fisted in her hair, slanted his head to hers and took the kiss deep. Way deep.

This time he knew she was ready. This time she groaned and leaned into him, kissing him back with a hunger that almost put him on his ass. His whole body tightened with each soft brush of her tongue against his. The top of his head felt as if it might just explode and for the first time in his life he felt as if maybe, just maybe, he could come from kissing.

He trailed one hand down to her hip, felt his rough hands catch on the silky material and stilled. She was freezing. She was near to naked and he'd been pressing her up against the cold metal of the truck. He lifted himself away from her. She'd been cold when she'd gotten into the truck, she might still be in shock, she could… Someone should kick his ass.

"Lily, this is…dumb," he managed.

What the hell did he think he was doing anyway? What the hell was *she* doing? He let out a rough breath. It was none of his business, right? Yeah, except that somewhere at the back of his mind, deep inside of him, he wanted to make it his business. It was dumb—really dumb—although at the moment, with the taste and scent of her on him, he didn't much give a shit. But maybe she would. *Later.*

Of the many kisses she'd experienced, of the few lovers she'd had, of the year and a half she'd been with Ian—no, wasted on Ian—Lily had never experienced anything like the sensations she'd gotten during those minutes of his mouth on hers, his body pressing into her. Or had it been only seconds?

She licked lips that felt swollen. He tasted like coffee, or maybe that came from her. She thought she'd been ready that second time, but when he'd taken control… She was still tingling from it. She took a deep breath and looked up.

God, his eyes.

They were dark, like everything else about him, but it was a deep-blue rimmed with a border of navy or black that made his gaze that much more intense. It was a look that saw everything in an instant and she shivered under his piercing stare, not from fear or even from the cold, but from something she didn't have a name for.

Where she'd gotten the courage to kiss him like that, she'd never know. She'd never done anything remotely like that before. She should have been scared, cautious at the very least, yet somehow knew she'd be safe with him. He'd done something extraordinary for her, knowingly risked himself for *her*, and it was weird, but she felt connected to him on some elemental level she couldn't even begin to understand. She was thankful, of course she was, but gratitude didn't have her heart racing, her stomach flip-flopping, her body singing. Did it? Jeez, who was she kidding? She ached in places that usually only came alive after long and intense stimulation of the solo kind.

All she knew was that she hadn't been able to just let him walk away. Not yet.

"C-Come inside," she whispered.

Yeah, and she so totally sucked at stuff like this.

When his gaze slid down to the juncture of her thighs, heat bloomed in her cheeks, low in her belly, between her legs.

"*With* me. I meant come inside with me. Although…" She took a deep breath and rushed on before she chickened out. "You can come inside me too. Well, we'll have to use protection, of course, but—"

"Lily." Gabe closed his eyes briefly and groaned.

"It's okay. You know, if you don't want to, I mean."

"God…"

His gaze slid over her in a hot caress resting on nipples she could feel hard and erect against the thin silk of her dress. Her stomach clenched. It wasn't exactly a "no".

She swallowed. She should probably give him fair warning. "You know." She licked her lips. "I-I've never done anything like this."

"Adrenaline," he dismissed. "It's just the adrenaline."

She shook her head. "No. I don't think so. I just..." She looked at him, tried to ignore the tremor in her limbs and went for it. "I've never wanted like this before. Never so quickly, but never, ever," she glanced away, "like this."

God, she probably sounded as if she had a screw loose or something. What happened to all that girl talk that assured a woman could get laid whenever she wanted, at the snap of her fingers? All of her friends had had one-night stands. Okay, they might not have been proud of them exactly, but they'd all expounded on the benefits of no-strings sex. After having the evidence that the relationship route hadn't exactly been working for her, didn't she deserve some uncomplicated pleasure herself? She was entitled, wasn't she?

His jaw flexed and his gaze bore into hers. He took a couple deep breaths. He seemed to be weighing his options. Jeez, she didn't want to have to twist his arm.

"I—"

"Why the fuck not?" he finally muttered.

The bottom dropped right out of Lily's stomach. Okay, not exactly the resounding response she'd been hoping for, but she could run with it, couldn't she? If she could get her nerves under control and didn't make a complete fool of herself, of course.

She frowned when he opened the passenger door and leaned in. His gaze was direct on hers when he straightened, a small square packet held unapologetically in his hand as if he wanted to be certain she saw it.

"Are you sure?" he rasped.

Her heart thundered, her throat was dry and the damn trembling was back. Especially when it registered he was holding more than one.

God, she hadn't been exaggerating when she said she'd never done anything like this before and she couldn't say why she was now exactly. Sex had always been a natural progression in the relationships she'd had. After a reasonable time, after getting to know someone, after feeling a connection that came with spending time together, but this… *This* was a driving, aching need, a want so powerful it drove her to seize the moment, to not let him just walk away and to hell with the fact she didn't know a thing about him. She just wanted to learn every inch of him, run her hands over the hard body she'd felt pressed against her, feel him on her, in her. She was drawn to him, her body attuned to his, every nerve ending tingling alive for him. And after knowing she'd wasted a year and a half of her life on a one-sided relationship, a farce, well, she was done with that.

She'd never gone for the bad-boy type before either. There was definitely something savage and untamed about him, something held tightly under control. He'd come tearing in, literally guns blazing and saved her from a fate that just might have been worse than death. It was hot and arousing. *He* was hot with this rough and rugged appearance, there was no doubt, but there was something almost vulnerable about him as well, something that reached out to her, as if he needed someone to keep him safe too. It was ridiculous. She knew it was. He was probably the last person who'd be in need of protection. He clearly didn't need it, wouldn't want it and probably wouldn't appreciate it.

Mouth dry, she nodded.

* * * * *

"Um…what happened to your face?"

My Goddamn knight complex.

At least that's what his cousins called it. He'd thought he'd stepped in to help the woman with an abusive boyfriend. Instead, she'd run to get five of his friends. They'd happily all thanked him for his interference...with their fists. Probably their feet. He'd sworn he'd give it up, that he was going to mind his own damn business and yet here he was with another "damsel in distress". At least no one had gotten killed and he wasn't going to get beaten up for his trouble this time. Nah, she wanted to screw his brains out instead. Made for a nice change.

Gabe shrugged. "Let's just say the last woman I rescued wasn't as appreciative as you."

Lily frowned, but before she could say anything else, he added, "So, where's the bed?"

He knew he was being deliberately crude and unfeeling but couldn't seem to stop himself. Part of him hoped she'd just tell him to go to hell because the rest of him wasn't capable of turning his ass around and getting out of there. He'd had some kind of serious reaction to her the minute he'd heard her voice and seeing her in person had amped it up almost out of his control. The brief kiss had just about blown the top of his head off and he wasn't even that into the whole kissing thing. After he got his hands on her... Well, all hell might break loose. He just wanted inside her, to lose himself in her sweet heat, to come with her wrapped around him. He yearned for that oblivion, even if it was short-lived.

He looked around the dim living room. Classy and elegant, just like her. He could smell fresh flowers and a clean he'd dreamed of for longer than he cared to think about.

"Of course, the bed's optional."

Yeah, he could be a prize asshole.

"U-Upstairs."

He followed, his gaze trained on the sway of her ass, as she made her way up the stairs and into a big bedroom. Oh yeah, he was sure of it. She had to be completely naked under the dress.

She kicked off the ruined shoes and flipped a switch, bathing the room in a low, soft light. Another surprise. He got a quick impression of a room decorated in soft, understated greens and not the over-the-top feminine luxury he'd expected. She stood next to the bed, hands clasped together. The stance had "second thoughts" written all over it.

"You can tell me to leave and I will. Right up until you get naked, of course, then I'm not sure I'll be capable of even hearing you."

He shrugged off his jacket when she continued to look at him and threw it over a sofa-chair in a corner of the room. His gut jerked when she licked her lips and her eyes followed the movement of his hands as he shrugged out of his t-shirt and tossed that as well. Still she continued to just stare at him, her eyes a little glazed.

She wanted him to make the first move? Do all the work? Well, all right then. He undid the button of his jeans, jerked open his fly and sighed in relief. Oh yeah. His hard-on was more than eager to be released from the stifling denim.

She swallowed and drew in a rapid breath. Her gaze locked on his chest as if she were fighting her eyes going lower. He looked down at himself ruefully and then back to her. He smiled. Yeah, he was giving her an eyeful.

"You...you should probably eat more," she croaked.

He choked out a laugh he hadn't been able to hold back in time. He knew he'd leaned down lately, but...not what he was expecting from her. Again. Jeez, why couldn't he peg her? He was an expert at reading people, he had to be, yet every time he thought he had her figured, she surprised the hell out of him.

"You know," he drawled. "When you see a guy naked for the first time? Especially his pride and joy? You should probably say something to stroke his ego. Something complimentary about the size of his dick would be a good start."

She swallowed again and her eyes skirted up to his. "Um…you probably know how built you are and I get the feeling you don't need any help with your ego, but ah, thanks for the tip."

What the hell had just happened?

He'd been ready for hard and fast and to be on his way as quickly as possible. He was still buzzed with the anticipation of seeing her naked, of feeling her under him, of getting inside her, but he felt some of the tension that was a constant sharp coil within him loosen ever so slightly. And he had the urge to linger, to learn her feel and taste, and to have her touch him. It'd been a long time since he'd allowed anyone to touch him, really touch him. Maybe he could even make her scream with pleasure. Yeah, he didn't think she was much of a screamer, but he realized he wanted to take on the challenge. He was definitely *up* for it.

Gabe shook his head. Man, maybe he really was losing it. He was here for a quick fuck, at her invitation, that was it. Nothing more, right? The big eyes, the uncertainty? They were an act, they had to be. If she wanted to play it that way, play *him* that way, well okay. He didn't really care for it, but if that's what she wanted, what she needed to get off, he was happy to play along.

He walked to her and took her hand in his. Her skin was soft and cool to the touch, but still gave him a searing jolt he felt deep in his gut and down into his balls. He pushed her palm flat against him and into the opening of his fly, pressing her hand to his aching cock and everything in him jerked at the contact. He barely bit back a groan and he was suddenly fighting the almost overwhelming need to close his eyes at the intensity of it. When the hell had that ever happened?

Oh God, oh God…

Lily repeated the litany to herself—over and over—although it was difficult with the sound of her heartbeat thundering in her ears and a shaft of *something* that speared between her legs. He was powerful but lean, his jeans hanging loose on slim hips as if he'd recently lost weight. She could see each defined line of muscle on his large frame. If he had some bulk, he'd be seriously huge. God, it...*he* was big and thick, hard and so hot against her palm. She felt the slight rasp of his hair against her sensitive skin and concentrated on trying to draw in enough air to ensure she didn't pass out.

"Suck me."

Her breath caught in her throat. Okay, that might have been a near miss. Her heart jolted and then raced as if it were going to burst from her chest at any minute. He urged her down onto her knees in front of him and her stomach clenched with nerves, in apprehension, in anticipation. The submissive position should have offended her, should have had every one of her feminist sensibilities firing, but somehow it didn't. Besides, the view alone was worth it.

He pushed his jeans down a little farther and wrapped her fingers firmly around himself before he removed his hand. "Lick me. Suck on me," he urged again, his expression tight, his eyes hooded as he looked down at her.

Lily licked her lips and tried to control the trembling she knew he had to feel. His skin was smooth. It was almost like handling hot steel covered with fine silk. She'd never thought about a guy being beautiful *down there* before, but Gabe epitomized the word "male" as he stood looking at her, his legs spread in a stance that screamed confidence.

Her fingers clenched involuntarily around him and his eyelids flickered. Okay, not as unaffected as he appeared. She trailed her hand in a slow, experimental motion up and then back down his hot, hard length. She could feel the heat coming off him as she leaned in, the musky scent of him filling her senses. She licked her lips again and gave a tentative, soft lick to the flushed head. His sharply indrawn breath gave her the courage she needed to tighten her grip, take an unsteady breath and lick him as if she might an ice-cream with firm, long laps up his length, from base to tip. She placed her other hand against his hard thigh for balance and felt his muscles clench as she swirled her tongue around the ridge under the head.

His taste infused her senses and a shaft of stinging heat flared between her legs at the sensation of his hardness against her tongue. Lily stretched from her knees to try to align her mouth so she could suck him in, but he was tall, the angle wasn't ideal. She grasped him and closed her lips over him, sucking softly and pulling him into her mouth as far as she could. He flinched when her teeth grazed the side of his cock.

Ouch. "Sorry," she murmured. That probably had to have hurt.

Lily shifted position a little thinking she'd get a better angle, but regardless of what she did, or how she moved, it felt awkward. She felt awkward, her movements unsure and clumsy, inexperienced.

"It's good."

She licked up his length again and was relieved when he grunted softly. Okay, that'd work. Realizing she hadn't given his balls any attention, Lily slid her hand down and cupped them in her palm, shuddering at the sensation of his wiry hair against her skin, taking the opportunity to draw in some air as she weighed them. They were firm, his skin drawn tight, and she squeezed.

"Jesus. Easy," he gasped.

Maybe a little too hard.

He adjusted the placement of her hand with his own, his fingers moving around and under hers, coaxing, guiding. "Here. Like this."

All at once she felt the sting of tears at the back of her throat.

Dammit, she wasn't any good at this.

Hadn't she heard that enough times? Why did she think she could do this? She released him and got up, almost tripping when she stood on the hem of her dress. He caught her arm to steady her.

"I'm sorry," she somehow managed.

"Hey—"

"Ian always says—"

"I said it was good." He kept his hold on her when she would have swung away from him. "Is it the best I've ever had? No. It is the worst? Fuck, no. It was good. I was into it. And for future reference?" His voice hardened. "When you're going down on a guy? The last thing he wants to hear is another man's name."

There was that wounded look again. And the soft eyes.

God, she had to be playing him. No one who looked like her could be so lacking in confidence. Could they? Could she really be that shy? That inexperienced? That naïve? Or was it just some sophisticated act or game? If so, she was a fucking expert at it and he'd know. He'd lived the edges of civilization for so long he'd been witness to every game there was and he'd become adept at spotting artifice. His life had depended on it more than once.

Why the hell should he even care? She wanted to play the innocent, vulnerable damsel, bursting with gratitude that the big, rough hero had rescued her? To show her gratitude in a time-honored way? He should be thankful for his good fortune. Right?

She was involved with someone or had been and she wasn't his type, although he had no fucking idea what that might actually be anymore. There was a time when he wouldn't have thought of touching her, when he would have stayed clear, regardless the invitation or how tempted he was. Those days were long gone. Now he was conditioned to take when he could because tomorrow everything could go to shit.

He let his fingers trail from her arm and jammed them into his pocket, his gaze trained on her. He used his teeth to open one of the small square packets he'd taken out, his movements slow, deliberate. He'd have to remember to thank the guy who'd left his stash in the truck.

"I don't fuck uptight sorority types as a rule. This is not going to be some nice, gentlemanly fuck. Think you can handle it?"

She nodded and licked her lips. His overactive imagination had her savoring his taste and his dick twitched in reaction.

He actually got a jolt from his own touch as he smoothed the rubber down his length. Probably had a lot to do with the wide-eyed fascination he was getting from her.

He frowned. She reminded him of a defenseless chick and for a second he wanted to kick his own ass and leave her alone, but he wasn't that altruistic, not anymore. Not enough to turn down the chance to be all over her hot little body. It'd been a long time since he'd had a woman under him for more than ten minutes at a time. It'd been even longer since he'd had a woman of his own. The allure of her sweet body and womanly softness was more than even he could stand.

"And I like it hard and fast. You up for that?"

She licked her lips again, dragging her gaze up from where he was suited and ready to go. "You—ah—you said that already. W-Whatever you want, however you want it."

Gabe stilled. Where the fuck did she get off saying stuff like that? Christ, he could be anyone. She had no idea some of the things he'd done. It almost made him want to shake her for putting herself in such a vulnerable situation with a guy she didn't know a thing about—even if that guy was him. He mentally shook himself. Yeah, maybe he really was finally losing it.

"So lose the dress. And get on the bed."

Chapter Three

The trembling was back again. She hadn't been brave enough to just whip the dress off and stand before him without a stitch on. Instead, she'd sat on the edge of the bed and taken it off over her head, conscious of his dark gaze tracking her every move.

Yeah, really sophisticated, Lily.

She tried to stem it when he stepped to her, his cock held firmly in one hand, nudging her legs apart to make room for himself. And failed miserably when he leaned over her, bracing one hand on the bed beside her, forcing her to lie back. She could barely make her throat work as she swallowed at the sensation of rough denim rasping across the sensitive skin of her inner thighs.

Her first thought was that he wasn't even going to take the rest of his clothes off. Her second was...oh God, this was really happening. Right now.

She tried to focus on breathing as his hot gaze skated across her breasts, down her body and between her legs where she was completely open to him, held wide by powerful thighs. She only knew she succeeded because she was still conscious.

He pressed himself against her and she inhaled sharply, her heart beating so fast she could hear the thunder of it in her ears. The trembling had started in her thighs and there was nothing she could do to control it. She could feel the blunt heat of him even through the thin layer of latex as he guided himself, tracing up and down her folds, slowly but firmly. She swallowed at the realization he was coating himself with her moisture, preparing himself, and her body clenched involuntarily.

His body was rigid, every muscle standing out starkly on his powerful form when he stopped, poised at the entrance to her body. His jaw clenched. Those dark, intense eyes lifted and locked onto hers, stripping her bare, and the bottom dropped right out of her stomach.

"Say the word and I'm gone."

Lily might very well have panicked save for that offer. That and the way the words seemed forced out of him, the flush high on his cheekbones and the shudder he couldn't conceal that ran the length of his body. She could see the effort it was costing him, yet he waited. For her.

The low heat she'd felt since she'd first laid eyes on him flared between her legs, right where he rested against her. She wanted what she saw in his eyes, wanted it like she'd never wanted anything in her life before. She saw restraint, yet there was a hunger there, a hunger she'd never seen from anyone else as they looked at her. God, she wanted to know what he'd feel like buried deep inside her, what she'd experience as he held her down and pounded into her, what it would feel like to be his woman.

She took a shaky breath and shook her head, not trusting her voice.

His gaze held hers for an endless second and then dropped down again. She felt it—the width of him, the tightness of her own body and couldn't prevent the slight gasp when he eased his weight forward, pressing into her in a firm, relentless push.

Lily tried to ease tensed muscles, to calm the erratic breathing, the roaring of her blood, but only managed to gasp again as he rocked back and forth once more.

"It's okay," he groaned. "Relax."

Lily swallowed at the blunt pressure, squeezed her eyes shut and tried to do just that. She shifted her hips a little on the bed in a futile effort to ease his way, for a better angle, to help alleviate the feeling of fullness.

"Easy," he ground out.

She was holding herself taut in anticipation of his next retreat and entry. She could feel it, but for the life of her couldn't release muscles wound tight, nerves strung taut. Her body just wouldn't cooperate.

"Dammit."

Her eyes flew wide at the savage curse. Her breath caught at the reality of the man braced over her, her legs held wide by his own powerful thighs. His eyes were dark, glittering slits, his breathing harsh, the skin pulled taut across his lean cheeks.

"Sorry," she managed. "I'm sorry..." Her voice was thick, the back of her throat and her eyes stung with the effort.

Oh God. She hadn't even been able to touch him properly, had come off as a nervous, inexperienced idiot, and now this. Did she really need any further evidence that she totally sucked in the sex department, in the seduction department, in the *men* department? Her own fiancé had preferred to screw a nameless stranger in a bathroom at a party. She might have been able to brush off Ian's actions and blame him for not being able to keep his dick in his pants, but she couldn't even pick up a ready, willing and more-than-able guy for some no-questions-asked sex, sex that she just knew would have rocked. Not even when she'd burned and ached for him. God, she was hopeless, useless. Pathetic.

"No, I am," Gabe ground out, lifting his head, his chest rising and falling with deep pulling breaths.

She turned her head away, but not before he saw the moisture at the corner of her eye and all of a sudden he knew—it wasn't any kind of game.

Fuck.

"Someone should probably whip me for this."

This was by far the dumbest fucking thing he'd ever done. To think he could be with a woman like her, now, after everything that had happened. God, he was deluding himself.

"It's been two years for me, Lily." The words were forced from him before he could stop them, as if that could make up for anything.

"Two *years*?" She turned a shocked gaze back to him. "You haven't been with a woman in two years? How—"

He shook his head. "I've fucked when I needed to, when I had to. I just meant… I meant I haven't made love to a woman in over two years. Maybe I don't know how anymore."

He moved off and back from her, shivering when the cool air washed over the parts of him that had been pressed up against her. He didn't have any right to touch her. It felt as if he'd tainted something he shouldn't have, corrupted something he'd had no right to think could have been meant for him, even if it was just a brief roll in the sack. He welcomed the pain as he removed the rubber with several quick, savage tugs that ended in a stinging snap.

Served him right.

He jerked his jeans back up, wincing as the fabric scraped over an erection he knew wasn't going away anytime soon, and bent to pick up his shirt. He wanted to say something, anything, to make it better, to fix it so she wouldn't feel bad, wouldn't blame herself, wouldn't fucking *cry*, but all he could manage was, "It's okay. I'll go." He just didn't have the emotional bandwidth at the moment for anything more.

"Wait, don't…please. Gabe…"

He closed his eyes. God, how often had he craved the sound of his name, for someone, anyone to speak his name, just once in all those long months? Nothing else would have had the power to stop him in his tracks in that instant, especially when he'd made up his mind that the best thing he could do for her was to get out of her sight as fast as possible.

"Stay," she whispered.

"Why the hell would you want me to stay? After that disaster?"

Lily sat up on the side of the bed. "I've never done anything like this before—"

"Yeah, I got that." The evidence had all been there, he'd just chosen to read it the way it suited him and he should know the fuck better than that. After all the practiced and insincere sex he'd had, he was drunk on the knowledge of it now. Too late.

She swiped at the wetness on her cheek. "I'm sorry, I know I'm not very good at this kind of thing, but I—"

"Jesus, don't apologize to me." He bent to her so that he could see her face clearly, so he could be sure she knew he was dead serious. "You're beautiful, generous and so fucking responsive, I— It's nothing to do with you. Nothing. I can barely stand to live inside my own skin these days. I don't know what the hell I was thinking. Clearly I wasn't." He straightened away from her and thrust an arm savagely into his t-shirt. "It's on me, okay? It's all on me."

"So...don't go."

He froze, swallowing at the lump in his throat when she stood.

It wasn't bragging to say he'd seen a lot of naked women in his life—beautiful and sexy naked women—so why did the sight of her standing in front of him without a stitch on have his breath catching and his heart racing? Why did he have to clench his fists to keep from reaching out to her? Sure, she had curves in all the right places and full, rounded, gorgeous breasts, but did that really justify a reaction he might have expected from a horny kid?

"Lily," he groaned.

All at once she was standing so close to him, he could take a deep breath and he'd probably brush against her nipples. "I'm not much used to slow anymore. I..."

"Stay. Make love with me, Gabe."

God, he wanted to. The look in her eyes made his stomach twist. He saw the doubts, the uncertainty and knew he'd put them there and he hated himself for it.

He swallowed as he raised a hand, threaded it through her soft hair and cupped the back of her head. Everything in him screamed to grab onto her and drag her into him. He fought the urge, but it was a close call.

With a thumb he tilted her jaw up and bent to put his mouth over hers. He moved slowly, wanting to give her every chance to pull away yet all she did was lick her lips, open her mouth and close her eyes.

Aw, man.

He groaned as her mouth opened under his, eager, hungry. She pushed herself forward until she was flush against him and a shiver chased through him that had nothing to do with the cold and everything to do with a raging lust he wouldn't have thought possible. No, that didn't sound exactly right, but whatever the fuck it was it had him shaking as if it were his first time.

Her arms came up across his shoulders and threaded into the hair at the nape of his neck, her fingers clutching at him. Another shiver coursed through him at the sensation. As he thrust his tongue against hers, he ran his palms up and down the silky skin of her back, over her firm buttocks and back again in smooth sweeps. God, she was so soft. His hands must feel as rough as sandpaper to her. He groaned at the shock of her breasts against his chest when she leaned into him even more, plastering herself to him. He skimmed his palms up her sides to the curves of her breasts, easing his hands between their bodies to cup and squeeze.

Oh, fuck yeah.

She trembled and whimpered into his mouth.

They were all natural. As if he'd had any doubt.

She thrust her hips against him—in a way that said she probably didn't realize what she was doing—and that just made it all the more hot.

All of a sudden he couldn't concentrate, couldn't kiss her and touch her at the same time and he wanted—needed to touch her. Like he needed to breathe. He lifted his lips from hers, his breathing heavy. Her eyes were a darker green, glazed with hunger as her lids slowly lifted, her lips red and swollen and he felt himself harden further. God, how was that even possible?

He eased his hand down between her legs and cupped her heat with a firm hand. She was neatly trimmed, the soft hair tickling his palm, and smooth and silky down between her legs. He smiled savagely to himself when she jerked and whimpered against him. *There.* He felt it against his fingertips, his palm. Now she was wet, more than wet for how he wanted to do her, for what he wanted to do. He gritted his teeth as he stared into her eyes, rubbed a fingertip along her folds then eased his middle finger inside. Her eyelids flickered as he slid into her wet heat with a firm glide and he felt the clasp of her body around his finger.

Oh yeah.

"Gabe..."

He let out an unsteady breath as she tipped her head back with a moan that sounded as if it was forced from her. God, she was so fucking beautiful.

He thrust in and out of her slowly, fucking her with his finger, savoring the snug heat and the way her breath caught each time he pushed in. Her eyes were closed now, her mouth open slightly as she panted. Heart thundering in his ears, he used the pad of his thumb to brush against the nub of her clit in time to his thrusts and had to clench his jaw at the way she clutched at his shoulders, at the jerky movement of her hips against his hand. His jaw ached with how hard he was clenching his teeth.

She was close.

He would have liked nothing better than to make her come like this, yet the roaring in his head demanded he take her. He wanted to sink himself inside her all the way to his balls, as deep as he could get. *Now.* He flexed his hand, rubbing the heel of his palm against her mound as he withdrew his fingers slowly.

He felt the wetness on his fingers, his hand. The scent of her arousal hung in the air, but he resisted the urge to lift it and smell her, to put his fingers to his lips and taste her. Barely.

Need and hunger raged at him. He wanted to touch her everywhere, do everything to her all at once, he wanted to slide into her and pound against her until he exploded, until they both did. And he wanted her mouth on him again, almost more than he wanted to draw his next breath.

"I want… God, how I wish I could fuck you and have you suck on me at the same time," he groaned as her heavy lids lifted.

Lily jolted and gasped. She couldn't help it. The explicit images were right there, coming at her too easily in blazing color. Oh God, he couldn't possibly— How could he have—

"Like that idea, huh?" His gaze became molten. "Two cocks?"

"No, of course not." She could barely focus, could hardly think with what he'd been doing to her and he wanted to talk deep, dark desires? "I mean, I-I never would. I wouldn't want to, for real, *ever*." But it was her private fantasy, the one she thought about in the secret recesses of her mind, the one she would never, ever think to act on, the one she wouldn't have revealed to anyone, yet it was somehow out there. "I…"

"Show me your vibrator."

"My *what*?"

Lily let her hands slide from the muscled slopes of his warm shoulders. She was pretty sure she'd passed the point of being able to pretend any kind of worldly sophistication, but she thought she'd give it one more shot just the same.

She cleared her throat. "What makes you think I even have one?"

He smiled. It was wicked and full of knowledge.

Yeah, that was probably a fail.

"I bet it's top of the line. Dildo-vibrator combo, right? Real lifelike. Probably a lot bigger than your boyfriend. You think about him when you use it or about someone else giving it to you?"

Lily swallowed. She was pretty sure from here on out it would feature him—front and center—and in vivid color.

He glanced around the room. "You probably keep it close, right?"

Lily shivered when he stepped from her, but he grasped her hand and led her back to the bed, urging her down.

He reached over and opened the drawer of her bedside table. He smiled at the silky pouch he pulled out before jerking the strings open.

Her heart pounded as she watched him weigh it in his hand. He'd been so spot-on, it was uncanny. It was an expensive model, shaped and colored to exactly resemble an atomically correct, beautiful cock, even down to ridges and raised veins and the heavy balls beneath. It was made of a special silicon that gave it a realistic look and feel. And it was larger than Ian. Not mammoth, but any guy with a cock that size would be forgiven for prancing around. Gabe might even be a little bigger.

"You got some lube?"

Lily licked her lips. "Gabe..."

The protest sounded feeble, even to her. Her entire body was on fire and the muscles deep inside her clenched when he raked a hot glance over her. She was wet, her body throbbing in memory of how his finger had felt inside her and now he was going to—

"Lie back."

Oh God, she'd practically begged him to stay, hadn't she? All right, there really was no "practically" about it, but this wasn't exactly what she'd had in mind. The aching burn that radiated between her legs and chased over her entire body didn't seem to care one way or the other.

Lily made herself as comfortable as she could. Her throat was so thick she could barely swallow as he helped himself to the small tube she also kept in her bedside table. Watching a guy smooth lube on her vibrator? Talk about being outside her comfort zone.

He came down onto the bed, big and gorgeous with his smoothly muscled, bare chest and unbuttoned jeans. He was still partially visible in the opening. And hard, really hard.

Oh God.

Her stomach jolted and she jerked a little as he urged her legs apart to make room for himself and placed the head of the vibrator between her legs. That first contact almost made her forget how exposed and open she was to his gaze. Almost. She licked lips suddenly bone dry as he moved it slowly up and down her folds and she focused on simply trying to breathe.

"I'm guessing you've got it on the setting you like, right?"

"Gabe..."

She lost what she'd been about to say as he flicked the switch and the vibrating head nudged her clitoris. Sensation speared from between her legs, exploded low across her back and abdomen and down each limb. He did it again and again, until it was an effort to keep her legs still, her hips from thrusting off the bed and from moaning her head off.

"Watch," he urged. "I want you to watch."

Oh God.

His gaze was fixed between her legs and the expression on his face… She was sure no one had ever looked at her like that before. She levered herself on her elbows with an effort and glanced down a body racked with need.

He nudged her inner thigh and then eased the thick length into her in a slow, firm push. It was all she could do to keep her eyes from rolling back into her head. She was so hot, so swollen and already so wet, it sunk into her and she did moan. She moaned and shivered at the sensual pressure.

"Jesus, look at you."

Lily gasped. In and then back out, almost all the way. It had never felt even half this good when she used it. And all at once, even if she'd wanted to, there was no way she could keep her hips still. She heard herself panting and gasping, but was beyond caring what she looked or sounded like.

"Christ," Gabe muttered when she arched off the bed.

He flicked his thumb over the nub of her clitoris and Lily gripped the covers by her sides in fists clenched tight. The sensations akin to falling, yet she was lying down, zinged up and down her entire body, radiating from between her legs.

"I want you to take me into your mouth."

"Gabe…"

"Close your eyes."

She was having trouble breathing, couldn't seem to get enough air. It was overrated anyway, right? God, she wanted to take him into her mouth, to taste him as the thick length moved in and out of her body. She closed her eyes. She could almost imagine.

"There's two of us," he whispered. "Maybe brothers…yeah, brothers. We've been fighting over you, over who gets to be with you. We both want you so bad. We think…maybe we both can."

She was going to go up in flames.

"He got to fuck you first and it drove me crazy to watch you with him."

She let out a shaky breath as she felt the bed dip beside her and then he nudged her lips. With his cock. She trembled and opened her mouth, slowly drawing him in, her lips closing around him, sucking him gently as he thrust carefully in and out.

"Oh yeah, baby, that's it. Look at you. You're pleasuring the both of us."

Lily shuddered. He was still thrusting with the vibrator and she could almost believe there were two men, wanting her, sharing her. Oh God, she'd never felt so carnal, laying back with one cock sliding in and out of her body, the other in her mouth. Two cocks. Two guys. Finally she couldn't continue to suck him, not if she wanted to keep her sanity. The intensity of the pleasure he was wringing from her body wouldn't allow her to focus enough for that anymore. She was close, so close to her body exploding and all of a sudden she didn't want it, not like this. She groaned as she pulled her mouth from him, dragging her eyes open with an effort.

"No." She reached down, clasped his flexing forearm. "No, please...*stop*," she managed, trying to control the movements of her hips, to prevent herself from going over, but rapidly losing the battle.

He stilled. Heavy, dark eyes lifted to hers. His skin was drawn tight over flushed cheeks, his mouth a hard slash of need. Every muscle was etched in relief on his lean form and he was breathing deeply, harshly.

"Not like this, I want it to be with you inside me."

"Lily," he groaned.

She pushed against his arm, urging him to draw back. She gasped as the bulbous head slid from her. Her inner muscles contracted, clenched at the loss. She felt empty and balanced on the edge of something she somehow knew was going to be different than anything she'd ever experienced before.

"*You.* Come inside me. *Hurry.*"

He paused for an endless second before exploding into motion, standing up to toe off his shoes and socks, jerking his jeans down and off and kicking them aside. Oh God, completely naked he was breathtaking. She could feel how wet she was, and the stinging ache between her legs amped up to almost pain as he ripped open another packet with his teeth. A shudder passed through her body at the sight of him touching himself, smoothing the latex down his thick cock. And then he was kneeling on the bed, positioning himself between her legs, nudging her legs wide with his powerful hair-roughened thighs.

She tried to catch her breath as she looked up at him, tried to calm the thundering of her heart, the roar in her ears, but all she wanted was to feel his weight. On her. *In her.*

He was poised against her. She could feel him. One push and he'd be inside her.

"Are you sure? Lily, be sure." The guttural words sounded as if they were torn from him.

"Are you kidding? Now? When I'm more than ready? When I'm—"

"I wouldn't leave you, I mean, I'll make you come, I'd be happy to, but we don't have to, *I* don't have to—"

"Gabe, now," she cried. "Please…"

He folded himself down over her, his legs opening her wider, his forearms resting next to her head as he looked straight down into her eyes. His jaw flexed before he thrust into her in a long, deep stroke that took him all the way in. She cried out, heard the sounds, threw her head back, closed her eyes tight and grasped at his hard shoulders to try to anchor herself in a world that was suddenly only molten sensation. Her entire body vibrated with the hot length of him like a brand inside her, the feelings so acute she suddenly wondered if she was going to be able to survive it.

They groaned together when he began to move, smooth, sure movements that catapulted her body into stimulation overdrive and seared her all the way to the soles of her feet with each pump. She was so close—

She gasped when he flipped them over and she suddenly found herself draped over his hard, hot chest.

"Sit up. I want to see you," he demanded. His voice was deep, rough.

Lily tried to open eyes that felt too heavy to respond. She pushed herself up shakily until she was braced above him, her hands splayed across his chest, her knees on each side of his lean hips. He was lodged deep inside her.

And he was so beautiful stretched out beneath her.

"God, look at you."

"I..." She cleared her throat when her voice came out husky. "I was just thinking the same thing."

He raised his hands above his head, the muscles of his biceps bulging as he gripped the headboard. His gaze moved down her body slowly and then back up to meet hers.

"Move, Lily."

Her stomach jolted at the harsh command. She flexed her hips and gasped as he moved inside her. She eased herself forward and back, up and down as far as she could, gasping at the sensation of him rubbing against her clit. She could feel the thunder of his heart under her palms, yet he was only helping her with slight movements of his hips and they seemed to be something he couldn't control.

"Gabe."

She was close, so close, but as much as she tried, as much as she moved, she couldn't get the angle, the rhythm right. She was balanced on a knife edge of need again, just out of her reach. Frustration hammered at her.

"Gabe. Gabe...*help me*."

"Nah." He shook his head slowly, his gaze making slow sweeps of her face, down across her breasts and lower to where their bodies were joined. "I like it."

Lily took a deep breath, sinking down onto him and sending him deeper inside her. Her clitoris throbbed, she ached, her muscles strained and contracted around him.

"You like that I don't know how to do it properly?" she managed.

His eyes were heavy lidded. He lowered his arms and ran his rough palms up and down the tops of her thighs, easing her rigid muscles. She trembled at the look in his eyes.

"Yeah, I do."

She started to get up, but his hands clamped down onto her legs. He wasn't holding her roughly, but she couldn't move without some major effort.

"You're driving me wild with those moves."

Lily looked down. She slid one hand down his chest to his flat abdomen and his muscles flexed under her touch.

She swallowed. "I am?"

"Oh, yeah," he breathed.

He reached up, wrapped a rough hand around the back of her neck and brought her down flush against him, chest-to-chest, face-to-face. The movement caused her nipples to brush against his chest and his cock to ride up hard against her clit. She inhaled sharply. His gaze roved every detail of her face, his thumb traced the contours of her lower lip and she shivered. He angled her head and put his mouth against her neck in a hot, opened-mouth kiss that had her grinding her hips against him and gasping for air.

His hands splayed across her buttocks, his fingers sliding between her legs close to where they were joined, holding her open for him as he began to move—long, forceful, deep thrusts.

"He's watching us again," he rasped into her neck.

Lily gasped as he thrust faster, her forehead falling against his shoulder as he held her hips steady for his entry and retreat.

"You're so wet from being fucked by him, so hot," he groaned. "But he didn't make you come. It's his turn to watch, but he can't just watch. He moves closer. He's got his dick in his hand, jerking off while he watches us."

Lily gasped at the images and just like that she was right back in the fantasy again. Two men, both focused on her and her pleasure—wanting her, needing her, sharing her.

"He wants another turn, but your sweet pussy's all mine, baby," Gabe growled.

He slid a hand between her legs and rubbed his fingers gently over skin drawn taut around him and up to the puckered entrance beyond, taking some of her moisture. Lily's breath caught.

"You ever been taken here before?"

She could only shake her head, barely able to concentrate on his words with the relentless entry and retreat of his body in hers barreling her toward something she could only helplessly wonder at.

She bucked against him when he applied slight pressure, driving her farther down against him and he groaned.

"Like that, do you?"

Did she?

He rubbed his finger lightly back and forth against her, tantalizing sensitive flesh as he continued to drive inside her in long, deep movements, holding her hips immobile, so that all she could do was accept his heavy thrusts, welcome them, anticipate them.

"He wants to take you here."

"Gabe," she gasped.

"It's okay," he whispered roughly in her ear. "I'm not letting him fuck you again. But I'll let him fantasize about it, about you. He wants inside you so bad though, wants to fuck you while I am, both of us giving you pleasure, making you come, together."

Lily screamed as the orgasm ripped through her, burning between her legs in a raging force and radiating throughout her entire body with a strength that shocked her. It was so intense, bordering on pain, washing over and through her as he continued to thrust, hard and deep.

She was vaguely aware of Gabe groaning under her, his breath sawing in and out, his arm rigid across the back of her waist as his body jerked against hers.

"You're incredible," he breathed when her movements finally stilled.

She still felt him, hot, hard and insistent inside her and frowned as she lifted her head.

"You didn't orgasm," she managed, her voice hoarse.

He smiled. "Baby, men don't orgasm. They come. And I did. I have a lot of pent-up, ah, adrenaline still to work off."

She licked her dry lips. She'd been completely unaware, but her throat felt as if maybe she'd screamed. "So, does that mean…"

"Yeah. It means I'm not done. Adrenaline can be a real bitch."

Chapter Four

"Lily, thank God. I've been worried sick. Where's the car?"

What had she ever seen in him?

Ian appeared weak and whiny, pale and almost frumpy in his perfectly pressed khakis and designer polo shirt. She should have been terribly hurt, she should be feeling a betrayal of the worst kind, she should be mourning the loss of what would have been. There should have been something, anything—instead, all she felt was somewhat detached and just...relieved.

She leaned against the doorjamb and crossed her arms over the loose robe she'd thrown on during her mad dash to the door.

"You've been worried sick about your car?"

Ian frowned. It was more than mild irritation. He hated when she did that, deliberately turned his words back around on him.

"Of course not. I—"

"Look, we don't have to drag this out or have it be more unpleasant than necessary. It may sound clichéd, but I really never want to see you again."

"Lily, please don't be hasty about this. I know you're probably upset."

Probably?

"It was unfortunate, what you saw—"

"It was unfortunate I saw it?"

He expelled a quick breath. "You think you're so darn smart sometimes."

No, she was stupid. How could she have been so stupid?

Lily turned at the slight noise behind her in time to see Gabe dragging on his jacket over the wrinkled t-shirt. He hadn't bothered to button the top of his jeans and her stomach jolted at the flash of smooth skin and rock-hard abs when he reached up to thrust his arm roughly into the sleeve. His jaw was darkened by a further day's beard growth, his hair messy as if he'd just run his fingers through it. He looked rumpled and so sexy, the flesh between her legs heated in memory of how deep he'd been buried inside her just a few hours ago. He was looking directly into her eyes with that intense way he had as he walked to her. It was the look that catalogued everything in an instant and you knew nothing had escaped his notice.

"You okay?" He pitched his voice low.

Lily nodded, not feeling she could trust her voice. She'd thought he'd left already. He hadn't been in the bed when the doorbell rang and she'd thought… Well, she figured she'd be dealing with the realization of what she'd done alone and that it was probably for the best. Now? Now she just wanted to taste him again, wanted another chance at his big, beautiful, thick length. And she wanted him inside her all over again.

"That last time, I—"

She licked her lips. "Fine, I'm fine. You don't have to leave," she added quickly, when he took his keys out of his pocket.

Gabe glanced behind her to Ian still standing at the door.

"Yeah, I do."

With the wrinkled clothes, black eye and bruised cheek, he looked like every mother's nightmare and just made her mouth water. God, just thinking what that lean body had done to her last night made her hot and shaky and wet all over again. And ready, she was so ready.

"Gabe..."

He took a card out of his pocket, ripped it in half and scribbled on it with a broken pencil he also took from his pocket. He thrust it at her.

"Here's my number. My personal cell."

"You could, ah, stay."

She knew it was pointless. It was a one-night stand, nothing more, right? Yet she couldn't help the words. Intellectually she knew she was still trying to come to terms with it, but she'd known what it was, hadn't expected more, yet...

"I have to get the truck back." He glanced behind her again. "Look, I don't want to be used as leverage or payback. You do what you need to do. Call me if you want. Or not."

Gabe got a surge of something when he saw the whisker burns and the mark on her neck. Yeah, it'd been a while since he'd shaved on a regular basis. He felt a quick rush of regret. He hadn't meant to mark her, had been too far gone to be aware of it, but he couldn't help being glad something would remain after she'd washed him from her body. It had also been a long time since he'd done something that hadn't been coldly deliberate and with deadly purpose. What would she think when she discovered it for herself? He wondered if she had similar marks anywhere else and then mentally kicked himself for not taking the time to find out—but he'd been shocked. He'd woken up completely wrapped around her. It'd been years since he'd spent the entire night with a woman, and even then, he'd never slept so deeply. He must have fallen asleep right after the second time—a deep, dreamless sleep where he'd been totally unaware and completely vulnerable. It'd thrown him so much that he'd forsaken the last remaining chance he was ever likely to have to look at her or touch her.

Moron.

He'd tried to hold himself back last night, to watch her through the sex as he always did, but Lily's response had been so open and unguarded, so fucking honest, and it had completely unraveled him. He'd had no choice but to give himself over to it and for a split second he'd been unaware of his surroundings, oblivious to everything and anything else. And well, that just scared the hell out of him.

He'd meant to leave before she'd woken, yet he'd found himself walking through her house, looking at her things, seeing the evidence of *her.* And he hadn't meant to leave her with a way to contact him, so why the fuck had he just handed her his number?

He glanced behind her, reached for the tie of her robe and tightened it. He had no idea where the urge came from. It was dumb, he knew it was, but he hadn't liked the thought that she'd been talking to another man when her cleavage was so exposed where her robe had loosened. The guy standing at the door had probably seen a hell of a lot more of her than he had, had touched a hell of a lot more of her. The knowledge burned deep in his gut, but he pushed it ruthlessly to the side. He didn't have any rights where she was concerned. She wasn't his and had no chance of ever being his, so what the hell was he doing fighting an overwhelming need to stake a claim? It wasn't like him.

He took one long, last look before he turned away and stepped past her. Damn. The tousled, just-rolled-out-of-bed look suited her. Too much.

He stopped in front of the guy who looked as if he weren't used to waiting for anyone and felt the cold, expressionless shield come down over his features. He more than welcomed it this time. Every instinct he possessed told him the guy wasn't the violent type, but it couldn't hurt to make sure.

"Lay a hand on her and I'll hunt you down like a fucking animal and break both your arms." It was a savage vow, delivered with deadly calm and had the desired effect. Gabe felt a spike of pleasure when he paled and turned to look at Lily.

"Who is this and is that a *hickey* on your neck?"

He imagined her lifting a hand to her neck in shock, probably dismay. Yeah, she wasn't likely to be pleased he'd left such a mark on her.

"Maybe. Probably."

Gabe's dick twitched at her slow drawl and he chanced a glance at her as he stepped onto the sidewalk. She didn't look or sound pissed at all. In fact—

"So, what did you do?" The guy's face went tight, his cheeks flushed. "Pick up some guy off the street and sleep with him to get back at me? Is that it?"

Yeah, Gabe had come to pretty much the same conclusion. What other explanation was there? She looked like a fucking princess, lived in a multimillion dollar tower and was engaged to some dude who could have stepped off the pages of one of those fancy men's magazines. The guy was seriously put together and obviously rolling in it. Of course, with a woman like that, there was always a man. So what the hell had she been doing with him? Slumming? What the fuck had she been thinking letting him all over her? He glanced back at her one last time as he reached the truck. He figured she'd be too distracted to notice, but she was looking right at him, her hand up against her neck.

He swallowed as he swung himself up into the cab. Damn, what one look from her could do to his body. He reached down and adjusted himself roughly as he started the engine. Well, his body just better get with the fucking program because he was never likely to see her again. Yeah, but there was still part of him that hoped that she'd think about him, remember him, at least for a while. *Dumb.*

She turned back to Ian once the truck was out of sight.

"Look, why don't you just go? It's over."

There was affront and anger, frustration and impatience, but she couldn't miss the glint of speculation as he looked at her and it made her sick. Secretly, deep down, she'd always thought their sex was a little boring, perhaps missing something, but had always assumed it had to do with her. After all, Ian had dated a lot of beautiful, sexy and successful women before her. She'd even deluded herself into believing it'd get better once they were married and were actually living together. She'd thought the greater intimacy… God she'd been such an idiot.

"Lily, please, I figured you'd need some time with this, but I— What did you expect me to do? She was all over me, I—"

"What did I expect you to do?" she choked. She crossed her arms again against the early morning chill. "How about saying 'no thanks'? How about remembering you have a fiancée? How about keeping your damn pants zipped?"

"She's a slut, she—"

"You're supposed to be a hot-shot defense attorney and that's the best you've managed to come up with?"

She'd thought to throw his own selfish and inept sexual prowess back in his face now that she knew what she was capable of physically, what Gabe had shown her she was capable of. Now she just wanted to get beyond it and have him out of her sight.

He cleared his throat and glanced to where Gabe's truck had been parked. "I'm willing to overlook—"

"Grow some balls, Ian," Lily almost sputtered. "Take responsibility for your own actions, admit you fucked up and let's move on."

She got a jolt of satisfaction when his eyes went wide at her language. Actually, the jolt may have come from simply saying the bad words. Out loud. She smiled. Wow, she hadn't even stuttered.

He frowned. "What's got into you?"

Lily laughed. She couldn't help it. She knew what had gotten into her, over and over last night. She still tingled and ached from it and she'd never felt so alive.

* * * * *

"Dammit, Lily. Don't you know how dangerous it is to open a door without knowing who it is first?"

As soon as the words left his mouth, Gabe could have kicked his own ass. She'd barely gasped his name when she'd swung the door wide before he'd let her have it. And she'd clearly been expecting someone else. Probably anyone else but him.

"It's a safe area."

"Sorry," he muttered.

Yeah, he'd forgotten. He'd forgotten there were still people out there who believed they were safe in their own homes, so safe they became complacent about it. She probably thought only bad things happened at night as well. God, to be that naïve.

"Um… Did you forget something?"

Yeah, to run his hands all over her one last time. He was staring, he knew he was. She was still wearing the robe, the one she'd had on earlier, but she'd showered. He could smell her fresh, clean scent. It wasn't overpowering, but made him lightheaded all the same. Her pale hair hung in soft waves around her face, a face bare of any makeup and she looked…real. Pretty. He swallowed. He could see the faint shadow of her nipples through the thin fabric and hadn't been able to miss the soft jiggle when she moved. Maybe she had a thing against underwear.

He shouldn't be here. It was dumb, he'd known it was. She was fine, she looked fine. He swallowed. More than fine. Every instinct he had said she hadn't been in danger from the pretty boy this morning, yet he hadn't been able to let it go. Besides…

"You called me."

Even though she'd hung up each and every time.

"Yeah, um." Lily wet her lips. "You knew it was me?"

He wasn't about to admit that apart from his family, she was the only one who had that number. Plus, he'd taken a note of her home number before he'd left anyway. Old habits die hard. She didn't need to know that either.

He shrugged and thrust a hand at her, palm up. He'd been fiddling with the thing in his pocket for hours. "You must have dropped this in the truck."

"Oh." Her hand flew to her ear. "I assumed it was gone. For good. Thank you, really."

The smile that lit her features and made her eyes sparkle almost caused his heart to stop. At least that's what it felt like. He glanced at the diamond earring. Yeah, probably another rich boyfriend showering her with things he'd never be able to afford. Assuming he still wanted to eat, of course.

She reached out and picked it up. Even though he was braced for it, he still felt a jolt all the way to the soles of his feet when her fingers brushed against his skin.

He cleared his throat. "I didn't thank you either. You know, for last night."

That clear gaze lifted to his and locked on.

"*You* wanted to thank *me*?"

Her voice came out a little husky and just like that he was hard—all the way hard—especially when her gaze did a scan of him from head to foot that said she was remembering him naked and in a good way.

He'd been going to do the noble thing, drop off the earring and leave, except doing the noble thing didn't come as easily to him as it used to. Yeah, just like last night. When he realized she hadn't been playing him, he'd been set on pleasuring her and then leaving—his own brand of apology, and in a bizarre way he thought he might have been able to make amends. Somehow. Yet she'd been so sweet, so open and he'd been so damn starved. The need had ridden him hard and he hadn't been able to walk away.

He wanted to ask her about the boyfriend, fiancé or whatever the hell that guy was to her, but the way she was looking at him should have been answer enough. He knew deep in his gut she wouldn't have been with him if she were committed to someone else and she sure as hell wouldn't look at him now as if she wanted all over him. Again.

He thrust both hands into the pockets of his jeans, thinking it might help with the urge to reach out to her. "So, ah, you guys back together?"

What was he doing? It was out before he knew it. Seems he wanted the words, after all.

She paused. "No. Seems he can't keep his pants zipped. It was news to me."

He frowned. "He was screwing around on you?"

Her lips tightened. "Last night. At a friend's party. I walked in on them."

Shit. Okay so that tidied up some loose ends. Looking at Lily now, knowing what it'd been like to be with her...the guy had to be a total dick. "So, if you're with a guy, you expect him to be faithful?"

What the fuck was he doing *now*?

She cocked her head slightly to the side and looked him right in the eye. "You think that's too much to ask."

He shrugged. "Some guys aren't made that way."

"I get that, but if someone asks you to marry him, tells you they want a future with you? I assumed it meant something exclusive, you know?"

He couldn't miss the thickness of her voice, but it wasn't hurt. It was the remnants of anger, pure and simple.

She pushed the hair back off one side of her face. "Do you...want to come in?"

The words were close enough to those she'd offered last night that a surge of heat went through him and burned low and deep in his gut.

Hell, yeah he wanted.

Man, he was so out of practice with this stuff.

"I thought we could…you know, maybe lunch…yeah, lunch."

As soon as the words left his mouth, he wanted to call them back. *Lame.* It sounded so fucking lame. If he wanted to get his end in again, it didn't have to be her did it? Any chick would do. Right? Besides, a no-questions-asked lay was one thing. There was no reason to think she'd be interested in anything else.

She licked her lips and he almost moaned when he saw that quick, pink tongue.

"I…" She looked down at herself. "I'd have to change."

The punch to his gut was quick and brutal. Even in the robe she somehow managed to look elegant. Gabe looked down at his shirt and smoothed a hand down the front. It didn't do a thing for the wrinkles he hadn't really noticed before. Damn, but he'd never felt so scruffy as he did standing next to her and he'd had his moments—plenty of them.

"Yeah, um, it's clean," he said, motioning to the shirt. "But it could probably do with an iron. You got one?"

"An iron?"

He smiled at the look of confusion, the line between her brows. It was cute on her. Maybe he should just plan to keep her off balance until he got her under him again. "Yeah, you know, it's an electrical device used to remove wrinkles."

She laughed and the soft sound had his dick twitching in response. "Okay, I have one of those. I have a fold-down board up in my closet. I…could do it for you?"

He looked at her as if she'd surprised him with the offer. Yeah, that made two of them. Every feminine instinct inside her protested, but she'd offered before she'd thought better of it. Maybe it had something to do with the slightly less than completely confident look she'd glimpsed. She didn't think he did vulnerable that often.

"Nah. Thanks, but my Mom made sure I could take care of my own stuff." Gabe quickly looked down at his watch, closed his eyes briefly and cursed. "Aw, shit."

"What's wrong?"

"I'm supposed to be somewhere."

"Oh, then—"

"Come with me? We can swing by there quickly, go grab something to eat and then..."

Just like that the bottom dropped out of her stomach. It could have been the eyes, locked onto hers almost as if he were watching for her reaction. More likely it was the images that immediately washed over her—or rather the echoes of sensation, pure and intense, that drove through her body like a hot stake. Pavlov, anyone?

"Jesus, Lily," he breathed. "Anyone ever tell you how easy it is to read your thoughts? You ever heard of playing hard to get?"

"You...you want me to?"

"No. No games." His voice dropped. "Not that kind anyway."

Lily trembled. She was still trying to calm the rioting of her senses at getting that first look at him and he had to go and say that? She'd reconciled herself to the fact she'd had a wild one-night stand, that she'd had mind-blowing, out-of-this-world sex with a guy she'd never see again. Or at least she thought she had, and now here he was saying stuff like that and every nerve ending had sat up to take notice.

She'd groaned when she'd heard the doorbell. She'd had enough with the phone calls all day pleading Ian's case, telling her he deserved a second chance, that she was being unreasonable. Her. Especially when they'd found out Ian's car and the ring were "gone". And her mother had had a fit. She expected Lily to overlook Ian's "indiscretion". After all, it had been what she'd done for Lily's father for years. It was a pity she didn't think Ian should have avoided the indiscretion in the first place, but she'd come to terms with her mother's view of things a long time ago. Having made no ground, she'd thought they'd decided the face-to-face route might be more effective. And she'd been in no mood for it.

But it had been Gabe instead. The first thing she noticed was that he'd shaved. The smooth line of his jaw only seemed to emphasize the dark intensity of his eyes and made the smudge of bruising on his face stand out.

He might be wrinkled, his thick hair sticking up in places, but it only made him look rugged, male, *hot*. Lily turned away before she went up in flames and shut the door behind him when he stepped inside. Immediately, she was aware of the heat washing off his big body.

She concentrated on controlling her breathing, deep, even breaths as he followed her with the silent way he had of moving—up the stairs, through her bedroom and into her closet. She tried to ignore the bed, the sheets and covers still a mess. She tried to ignore the images of what he'd done to her there, what he'd made her feel. And she tried to ignore her body—hot, wet and aching—wanting nothing more than to lay down for him again and have him do whatever he wanted to her.

It was all for nothing when she folded down the board, got out the iron and turned. Gabe was right behind her, unbuttoning his shirt and exposing an expanse of hard, muscled chest she knew she could never get tired of looking at. Or wanting to taste.

Her closet was huge. It had actually been another bedroom, yet it felt tiny, his large frame dominating the space. Oh God. He was here, in her space and the bed where he'd driven her wild and wrung a response out of her she'd only dreamed about was mere feet away. Not that she thought he'd ever necessarily need a bed…

Focus.

"Jeans. It'll be casual," he offered. His eyes dropped to her chest and her nipples puckered in immediate response. Had he noticed? "You might want to put on a bra."

Okay, make that a "yes".

Her cheeks heated. After all they'd done, after all he'd seen of her, touched of her, it should have been impossible, but it was as if his gaze were a physical touch. Her body reacted as if it were already conditioned to him and the stinging heat and moisture between her legs meant she was ready for him—in a matter of seconds.

She turned away when he shrugged off the shirt completely and laid it over the board. He had a little arrow of hair, just above the low-slung waistband of his jeans. She knew just how soft it was and she had to fight the urge to trail her fingers through it and follow it lower.

She opened her drawer and yanked out the first pair of panties she laid her hand on, conscious of Gabe watching her. Before she could push it closed, he'd stopped her with a hand over hers on the knob. Her mouth went dry.

"You got some serious panties here, Lily."

Lily swallowed and looked down. She had an entire drawer of them. A *large* drawer. Some women went for shoes or purses or even full-blown sexy lingerie sets. For her it was just panties. She loved all the colors and styles and she had quite the collection.

"I have a bit of a panty obsession, you could say."

"You think?"

She swallowed as he stepped into her, so close she could feel the warmth coming off his body, his half-naked body. He lifted his hand from hers and carefully sorted through them, checking out one after the other, rubbing the fabric between his fingers.

"These," he finally choked out. He gripped the white miniscule thong in both hands and gently stretched it out, looking at the demure panel on the front and then flipping them over to the back where there was a heart cutout. She wondered if he realized the little shape sat right at the top of the crack of her ass when she had them on.

"I want to see you in these."

Okay, he probably did.

Lily snatched the panties, grabbed up her clothes quickly and yanked out a bra she bunched in her fist. "I'll just, um…get changed in the bathroom."

Lily took a deep breath once the door was closed—a deep, shaky one. It was going to be a while before she got the image of Gabe holding her panties out of her mind. If ever.

She got ready in record time, conscious of Gabe on the other side of the door, imagining what he was doing, thinking. When she came out, he was dressed again, his navy button-down looking perfectly pressed. It looked as if he'd even tried to tame the wildness of his hair with his fingers and some of the doubts she'd begun to field melted away. Apart from the rugged maleness that clung to him, he was incredibly good looking.

Her stomach clenched at the look he gave her.

"What is it?"

With her hair left out and her makeup light, she looked good, she knew she did. His gaze started slowly from her brown ankle boots, up her legs encased in the dark skinny jeans she knew made her butt look good and over her breasts outlined in the thin, snugly belted metallic silver cardigan. It said he was slowly removing every item she'd carefully put on and had her right back where she'd been before—turned-on and not knowing exactly what to do about it.

"I've got my bike, but we can go in your car if you'd rather."

"Bike? As in motorcycle?"

His mouth kicked up at the side. "Yeah."

"I've never been on one before."

He smiled. "Then you're in for a real treat."

Chapter Five

"You liked it."

Lily shook her hair out and handed the helmet to Gabe.

"No," she laughed. "I *loved* it. I can't believe I've never done that before."

It had been an exhilarating experience and not just because of the ride. The feel of him between her legs, her thighs alongside his, her entire front pressed into his hard back, her hands clasping his lean waist, conscious of what lay just below her fingers…she wasn't likely to forget that anytime soon.

She looked at the front of the small, tidy ranch-style house they'd pulled in front of, the driveway and street littered with cars.

She frowned. "So, where are we?"

"Palos Verdes. It's an area between—"

"I know *where* we are, I mean what…"

He glanced back to the house, his eyes hooded. "My parents live here."

There was a funny feeling in the pit of her stomach. "We're here for a family gathering?"

"We won't stay long."

"Um, won't they think it odd? I mean…"

"Nah."

What was she doing here?

It wasn't the first time the thought had chased around inside her head. They'd had a chance encounter, a one-night stand. God, she still stumbled over the mere thought of it and she was going to meet his family? What did she really know about him? Her judgment had to be shot lately, perhaps it had always been.

"Gabe?"

"Yeah?"

She looked back to the house. "You, ah, don't really have a brother, do you?"

He smiled. It was one of his half-smiles, the one that had her weak at the knees and hot and wet between her legs in an instant. The one that had her recalling in minute detail the feel of his hot, hardness inside her mouth while he…

He caught a strand of her hair and rubbed it between his fingers, tugging gently, but just enough so that she was forced to step in closer to him.

"No," he murmured. "Just cousins. Five of them."

"Good," she breathed as his gaze dropped to her lips. "That could have been…awkward."

He laughed and she shivered as the sudden intensity in his eyes, her breath catching as he leaned in.

"Gabriel."

Lily jerked back and turned to see a crowd of people at the front door of the house. A small woman stood at the front, her hand raised to her mouth, her eyes teary.

Gabe grabbed her hand and pulled her with him to the door.

"Hey, Mom," he said quietly. "Happy Birthday."

"Oh, Gabriel," the woman exclaimed before wrapping her arms around him. She looked small and fragile folded against Gabe's powerful body. And then Lily became aware of the stares. Every set of eyes was on her. And there were a lot of them.

"Ah…I guess I must have some pretty bad helmet hair?"

"This is Lily," Gabe announced. There was a split second of silence before everyone started talking at once.

* * * * *

"What does she do?"

Gabe went still at the question from his father. He'd noticed Lily in deep conversation with a lot of his family since they'd arrived a couple hours ago. There'd been a lot of smiling and laughing. *Great.* It wasn't as if they'd had a lot of time to swap life stories and deep and meaningful aspirations. They all probably knew a hundred times more than he did about her.

It was ingrained in him though—the need to know, to understand, to always be aware of his surroundings and those he was with. He hadn't had much time when he'd woken up at her place, but it'd been enough to fill in a hell of a lot of gaps. And it had been a surprise, just another in a long line.

"She's a teacher. Elementary."

Yeah, he'd snooped. So what? He'd expected more high-profile, more glamorous, more in line with the house, the jewels, the car. Yet she was teaching at a public school and the more time he spent with her, well…

"She's classy, Gabe, real classy."

Yeah, that covered it. "And you're wondering what she's doing with me."

"Gabe…"

Gabe nodded toward where two of his cousins stood. "She'd be better off with one of them. With any of them. You know it and I know it."

His father sighed. "Well, from where I'm sitting, she's only looking at you, son. Even Zack hasn't been able to get anywhere with her."

"Zack?"

"Yeah, he has her baled up in the kitchen last I saw."

His cousin was smart, lethally smart. He was also better looking, a sharper dresser and had his shit together. *Fuck.*

"Been working on her for a while I think."

Gabe was already moving before his father had finished talking.

* * * * *

"So, you're all single," Lily drawled.

It was one of the cousins. Lily couldn't remember which one exactly. They were all tall, dark and way too good looking for one family.

He laughed and winked at her. "Yeah, we're hell on women. But that's the fun part."

She gazed into his incredibly blue eyes and placed her hand against his hard chest, giving it a gentle pat. She never would have had the nerve to do such a thing before last night. More likely she would have blushed and stuttered something dumb and dorky in response to a line like that.

"This approach usually work for you?" Lily asked in a husky voice.

"Huh?"

"Because to me it seems somewhat…unoriginal." She leaned in. "Besides, I'm here with Gabe. So…"

"So?"

"So, I'm with Gabe." Lily cocked her head to the side. "You guys make a habit of hitting on each other's dates?"

"Date, huh? Not girlfriend or woman, just date?" He looked her up and down. "You look much more my type, not Gabe's."

"Oh, and what might that be?"

"Where'd you guys meet?" he asked, ignoring her question and suddenly the light flirting seemed much more like an interrogation.

"Maybe you should ask Gabe."

"Yeah, he's not going to tell me."

The flirtatious teasing was gone in an instant. His expression hardened and a shiver of alarm had her pressing back against the wall behind her. He leaned in, close enough that she could smell the woodsy scent of his aftershave.

"Don't hurt him, okay?"

Hurt him?

Lily licked her lips and frowned. He'd issued the warning as if he really thought she could. "How—"

"Back off, Zack."

She gasped as Gabe launched himself into the room, that intense focus of his zeroed in on his cousin.

Zack backed up, his hands in the air as if in surrender and laughed. *Laughed.*

"She doesn't need you to come to her rescue, Gabe," he said. "She was just handing me my balls, all on her own."

Gabe stepped forward and took Zack across to the other wall, slamming him against it, rattling shelves and pictures. The savage threat was almost tangible.

"Gabe," Lily choked.

"What the fuck's got into you?" Gabe snarled. "You're forcing yourself on her?"

Zack looked at her as if he just realized he'd had her practically cornered with his body against the wall, braced over her.

"I was just… God, I'm sorry, Lily. I didn't mean—"

"Can't get your own women these days, Zack? You've got to come sniffing around mine?"

"If she looked at me the way she looks at you, what happened before wouldn't matter worth a damn, even if she'd been dumb enough to fuck you first."

Gabe frowned. "Don't talk about her that way."

Zack smiled, clearly unconcerned by the pissed-off threat still holding him. "You cuffed her yet, man?"

Cuffed?

Lily swallowed. She already knew Gabe was inventive, insatiable and generous in bed. God, was he into the kinky stuff too? And why didn't that do anything other than make her intrigued?

Gabe glanced at her and looked uncomfortable. He took his hands from Zack's shirt and stepped back from him.

Zack whistled. "She doesn't know you're a cop?"

"Was," Gabe snapped.

"*Are.* Always will be. Jeez, how long have you two known each other?"

"None of your Goddamn business," Gabe shot back.

She colored. She couldn't help it under the intense look Zack threw her way as he walked toward the kitchen door. Make that sauntered. He paused in front of Lily.

"Like I said, you seem more my type. Look me up when you're done with—"

Gabe stepped forward and snatched the card Zack held out to her before she could even think to reach for it, crushing it in his hand.

"What happened to the Goddamn pact?" he demanded.

Zack frowned. "Yeah, but you've never enforced it before. Ever."

"Well, now I am. And tell the others."

Zack put his hands up in mock surrender and with a crooked smile at her, reached out to shove Gabe's shoulder. For a split second they looked like a couple of kids, scuffling in the playground, until Gabe reacted with a move so fast it was a blur. He did something with Zack's hand and arm and had him back up against the wall, his forearm across the back of Zack's neck, Zack's arm bent up behind him.

Lily's heart pounded with the threat of violence, heavy in the air, aggression stamped onto Gabe's harsh features.

"Sorry." Gabe muttered something low and savage as he released him. "I'm on a hair trigger these days, Zack."

Zack flexed his shoulder as he turned. "You've got some new moves. You'll have to teach me that one."

"Yeah."

Zack rested his hand on the back of Gabe's neck. Being of similar height, they were pretty much eye-to-eye. "We've all missed you." His voice was deep. There was concern, wariness, as well as an obvious and deep affection between them. "It's good to have you home, but put some weight back on your skinny ass, okay?"

"What the heck was that all about?" Lily breathed as Zack finally walked off.

"Are you okay?"

"Of course. What was all that about a pact?"

Gabe shook his head. "It's dumb."

"Okay."

Gabe shrugged and smiled. "The six of us, we've always been competitive—toys, sports, girls. When we were in our early teens, we made this pact. We wrote it down and everything and we all signed it. No one hits on anyone else's girlfriend, date or romantic interest, if it's been declared. Hard-and-fast rule. It saved on blood being spilled and made our moms ecstatic. There'd been a fight every other week."

"Tell Zack he could do with some new material."

"Yeah?"

"Yes."

"So you weren't interested? I've heard he can be persuasive. Word is he's hot and the women really go for him. Of course, that's coming directly from him."

She smiled. "I can see the appeal, but," she lowered her voice, "I think you're much more my type."

He choked out a rough laugh. "Lily, I'm so far removed from your type, you have no idea."

"Why? Because you're a police officer?"

"Cop."

"There's a difference?" He didn't deny it this time, though it sounded as if he'd just corrected her.

He shrugged.

"And you drive a tow truck because…?"

"I'm taking some time. Trying to…" He let out a deep breath. "You've heard the expression 'good cop, bad cop'?" Gabe's voice was flat.

"Of course."

"I've always been good at playing the bad guy. Sometimes I wonder if I'm too good at it. It's why everyone thought I'd be good at undercover work."

"Undercover?" Lily's stomach clenched. "Sounds…dangerous."

"Yeah, it can be." His gaze lifted and locked onto hers. "I just came out of a deep-cover operation a few weeks ago."

She frowned. "Deep-cover? What does that mean exactly?"

"It means I'm undercover full-time, no contact unless absolutely necessary. I effectively become someone else for that period of time."

"Your family?"

"Yeah. No contact with family or friends. Too risky. Well, except for Zack and that was damn rare."

Lily swallowed. "How long?"

There was the slightest pause. "Two years. I've been…away for two years."

Lily heard the words as if from a distance. "Oh, Gabe. And this is the first time you've—"

"No. No, I— There've been a few visits, but it's been, you know…"

There's no way she could comprehend a scenario like that, have any hope of understanding what it could have been like, but it sounded so *lonely*. She knew now how it felt to be so terrified you could taste your own fear, to have adrenaline pumping through your body in such levels it was exhausting, to know what it was like to realize it was just you and that you were all alone, to face God knew what. And Gabe had been all alone like that for two years.

Lily put a hand on his chest and he tensed at the contact. She could feel the warmth of his body against her palm, the thud of his heartbeat. So vital, so alive. "There's no doubt you're a good guy, Gabe."

"Yeah?"

She'd seen his restlessness, the dark shadows in his eyes. Now she had some sense of what had put them there. "Absolutely."

He thrust his hand into the hair at her nape, his eyes dropped to her mouth.

"I feel good when I'm with you," he breathed before he tilted her head to the angle he wanted and sealed his mouth over hers.

His tongue eased between her lips in a bold, sure move, dominating her and a shaft of pure heat arrowed from her abdomen right down between her legs. A rough hand on her hip drew her against him and she groaned at the thick ridge nestled against her.

God, this man had seen her naked, touched her all over, his body had held hers down and she wished like hell in that moment there weren't any clothing between them. She wanted to feel his hot skin against hers, feel the slide of his hair-roughened legs spreading hers, wanted to feel his hot, hard—

"Shit."

Lily held back the whimper with an effort when Gabe lifted his mouth from hers. She drew in a shaky breath and when she managed to turn to see where he was looking, her face flooded with heat. God, she'd been ready to climb right up and onto his body—in front of an audience. Three more of his cousins stood crowded in the doorway, making no effort to hide their interest—or their appreciation of the show they'd been getting—if their stupid grins were anything to go by.

Gabe grasped her hand. "Come on. We're out of here."

Lily was mostly silent as they made their goodbyes. She had a different lens now in which to view their interactions and her heart ached for what this family must have endured. They were still wary of him, cautious, but there was deep affection in every word, in every touch, as they said their goodbyes to Gabe.

"Lily."

Gabe's mother hurried to her and folded her into a warm embrace.

"Whatever it is you're doing with him, keep doing it," she whispered in Lily's ear as she pulled back.

"What did my mom say to you?" Gabe asked as she reached the bike and he handed her the helmet.

She was surprised he'd noticed the low whisper. She smiled, all at once overcome with a naughtiness she'd never felt before.

"She told me to go screw your brains out."

He'd snagged a soda on the way out and she laughed when the mouthful he'd just taken sputtered all over him.

"*What?*" He coughed, wiping his mouth with the back of his hand.

She shrugged. "Well, she told me to keep doing whatever I've been doing with you, so…"

Gabe crushed the can and tossed it into the bin already on the curb. He shook his head, his eyes narrowing. It did nothing to minimize the heat that blazed from them. "I'm going to get you for that. You know that, right?"

Lily wanted to respond to the threat with a flirty "I can't wait", but his look was too raw, too filled with explicit intent for her to be able to get it out. All she could think about was how he'd exact revenge. And how much she was going to love it.

* * * * *

Gabe got a punch to his gut when Lily bent down and got a key out from under the mat. Her fucking front-door key. He glanced behind him. It was in full view of anyone who might happen to be on the street.

"Jesus Christ, Lily."

"I forgot my keys earlier since I wasn't driving. Besides, it's a safe area."

He shook his head and just watched her as she fit the key into the lock. He hadn't thought much about what he was going to tell people he'd been doing for the last two years of his life, but he knew it probably wasn't going to be the truth. Not all of it anyway. Yet he'd told her. Just like that and it hadn't exactly freaked her out. Of course, she didn't know all of it.

Riding with her practically wrapped around him had wound him up. *Tight.* He knew it was impossible, but he'd imagined he could smell her hot, sweet scent. It was all he'd been able to do to keep the bike steady to make it back to her place.

He'd never much cared about that stupid pact when it came to himself. A few had tried to goad him into fighting, but he'd always figured if a girl was more interested in one of his cousins than him, she should just probably go for it and he'd wish her luck. He'd never fought over a woman in his life, but the reaction he'd had when he'd seen Zack all over Lily had all but blinded him. He knew with everything in him that Zack would never have forced her, would never have hurt her, but he was still finding it difficult getting the image out of his head. And with another man's attention on her, it had hammered something home—that he hadn't taken his time with her last night, he hadn't even gone down, hadn't taken the time to touch, kiss or suck on her nipples, not the way he ached to now. If he felt a jerk before, now he felt like a real asshole.

The rigid control he'd held onto for dear life fractured the instant she closed the door behind them.

She gasped when he forced her backward until she came up against the wall with a slight thud. She was breathing heavily, her pupils dilated and she was drawing in air through lips slightly parted.

Oh yeah, he knew excitement when he saw it.

He put his hands on her—smooth, firm sweeps over snug denim, around her hips, down over her ass and back again.

She gasped. "Is this a-a cop thing? You want to frisk me?"

He laughed and swung her around before she had any idea of his intent. He grasped her hands behind her back with one of his own and pressed her front into the cool surface of the wall with his body. He leaned down to her ear and inhaled the sweet scent of her hair.

"Yeah." He kicked her legs farther apart with one of his feet. "With my tongue."

He felt the shudder that went through her along with the answering surge in his cock. How was that even possible? He'd thought he was already cocked and fully loaded. What was it about this woman that got him harder than he'd ever been before?

Man, those jeans made her ass look spectacular. He kept her hands locked in one of his as he knelt, taking his time skimming a firm palm up the outside of her leg, slow, sure. He cupped his hand over the rounded curve of her ass, fitting it to her shape, kneading the gentle slope. Unable to resist, he leaned forward and put his mouth on her, biting gently through the thick fabric, right where the sweet curve of her bottom met her thigh.

He let out a shaky breath when she jerked. God, he remembered he'd always loved that part of a woman's body.

He did the same to the other side. A whimper escaped her when he skimmed a hand up the inside of her thigh and cupped between her legs, his fingers easing along the seam and pushing up against her warmth.

Fuck. He swore he could feel how hot she was. He could only imagine how wet she'd be, with the way she was panting. He was so hard it felt as if he could split the seams of his own jeans, especially since he knew exactly what she had on under hers.

He pushed against her again with his fingers, searching for—

"Gabe."

And finding her clit. *Oh yeah.*

She moaned, thrust against his hand and he clenched his teeth in a futile effort to dim the roaring in his head. He shook with how badly he wanted her under him, with the images that rushed at him of her naked, wet, spread out before him as he pounded his aching body into hers.

He took a deep breath. Christ, he had to slow this the fuck down because he'd take his time this time, even if it killed him.

He eased her slowly around, grasped her hips and lifted, taking her weight, urging her legs up around his waist. Strong arms wound around his neck, her face turned up to his in invitation and he knew then she'd let him do anything he wanted to her. The realization rocked through him.

"Upstairs. We need to go upstairs."

He wanted a bed for what he had in mind and he needed to get there while he still could. Last night he'd been remiss, *seriously* remiss. Yeah, she'd come but he hadn't taken any time with her, certainly hadn't paid homage to a body that should have been worshipped. Jeez, had he really become such a crappy, selfish lover?

He made quick work of the stairs and sat down in the sofa-chair in her bedroom with her draped over his lap.

"So where were we?" he groaned as she settled her welcome weight onto his groin and the painful hardness of his dick.

"Ah." Lily cleared her throat. "If you're referring to downstairs, you were driving me insane with your hands but if you meant earlier, when we were interrupted, I believe you had your tongue down my throat."

He laughed and urged her forward until she rubbed along the thick, hard length of him.

"Gabe…"

He needed inside her in the only way he'd allow himself so he covered her mouth with his own and sunk into a kiss that spun the top off his world when she grabbed both sides of his head and kissed him back. Especially when she thrust her tongue forcefully against his.

He couldn't help his hips thrusting up against her and then she was grinding herself against him. Moaning and panting and rubbing back and forth and it hit him. She was close. He bracketed her hips with his hands and helped her, driving himself insane at the same time.

She threw back her head when she came, panting his name and clasping his hips between her thighs, her fingers clenching in his hair.

She finally dropped her head, resting her forehead against his chest, her breathing uneven. "God, I'm sorry," she mumbled.

He laughed. "Sorry? For *that*? Jesus, Lily do you know how hot that was?"

She lifted her head, her cheeks still burning. "Hot?"

He ran his hands over her hips and cupped her ass, pulling her into him tightly, smiling when she gasped. "Yeah. Feel that?"

He was hard and thick. It's what she'd used to get herself off. She couldn't have missed it and the look in her eyes said she didn't.

"Yeah, it was fucking hot."

Her hands went to the button of his jeans and he trembled—actually trembled—in anticipation and in frustration. He put a hand over hers.

"I want you to," he groaned. "God, how I want you to, but later."

Lily gasped as he tumbled her off him and began to throw off his clothes as fast as he could. His blood heated with her gaze following his every movement.

He grabbed the bunch of rubbers he'd stashed in his pocket, then lay back on the bed, wanting to make sure he had a choice view. Her gaze was riveted to his cock, long and hard up against his abdomen. It jumped when she licked her lips.

"Strip. But leave the panties on," he demanded roughly.

He smiled to himself. He had to hand it to her. She tried. He could tell she was self-conscious, a little nervous, as she tried to take her clothes off as seductively as she could. The awkward attempt made him ache for her just that much more and then suddenly she was naked except for the panties.

"Turn around," he choked.

Oh man.

"You are so fucking beautiful," he breathed. They looked exactly the way he'd pictured. The sweet curves of her ass cheeks were bare and the little heart cut-out sat right at the…

"Now, put me out of my misery. Take them off. Slowly."

She hooked her hands in the tiny straps on each side and skimmed them down with a little shake of her hips that almost had him embarrassing himself. At the last minute she turned and bent from the waist to take them off, giving him a heart-stopping, cock-bursting view between her legs.

He'd created a Goddamn tease.

Lily smiled as she straightened and turned, twirling the panties on her finger. She'd meant to fling them off into the corner, except somehow they flew toward him. He caught them right before they hit him square in the face. His gaze locked on hers as he drew them to his nose and her throat went dry. His eyes flickered as he inhaled deeply.

A growl rumbled from him that was her only warning as he surged off the bed, grasped her arms and had her spread out under him before she knew what'd happened.

She shuddered at the sensation of his hot skin pressed against her, at the look in his dark eyes as he drank his fill before lowering his head. She jumped when he bent and flicked a nipple with his tongue. She'd expected rough, God, she'd wanted hard, but it was a light touch. She whimpered as he licked her. Back and forth, wet and slow, over and over.

Helpless, she thrust her hips against him, grasped at his shoulders, trying to communicate without words that she wanted him. Inside her. *Now.* He didn't get the message. He just kept doing his best to drive her insane with need.

She reached down and wrapped her fingers around him, urging him between her legs.

Gabe gasped. "What's the rush?"

Okay that got his attention. "You like it fast, right?" she panted. "Now I do too. Please."

He drew a nipple into his mouth and sucked, hard, before he slid down her body licking and kissing as he went, dipping into her bellybutton and zeroing lower.

"Gabe."

She was forced to let go of him. Down he went, pushing her thighs wide with the bulk of his shoulders, exposing her completely to a gaze she knew missed absolutely nothing. It looked as if he were memorizing every detail of what she looked like. She took a shaky breath as he leaned forward and blew gently on her wet, stinging, aching flesh. His intent was stamped on his heavy features.

She gripped his hair. "You don't have to. I—"

"Yeah, I do. I've been seriously remiss. But I plan to remedy that, right now."

She swallowed against the constriction in her throat. "I'm ready, more than ready, you don't—"

"I know. I can see how ready you are. You're so wet. God, Lily, I have to."

He bent to her.

"Wait, I—"

"I can't."

His nostrils flared slightly and she swallowed again. The churning, twisting sensation in the pit of her stomach swirled out of control, the stinging ache between her legs a physical pain.

He spread her carefully with his thumbs and she shuddered. Her legs moved restlessly against the bed and he smiled savagely at the show of anticipation. He blew against her gently again and she jerked, she shook, she needed.

He lowered his head and licked her—right there—slowly, boldly with the firm flat of his tongue and she caught the faintest whiff of her own arousal as she dragged in a deep breath. He did it again and again, licking then sucking lightly. Then, oh God, he flicked at her with his tongue, back and forth—fast, even, relentless flicks she couldn't get any relief from, not with the way he was holding her hips.

She gasped and bit her lip and fought against the urge to grab his head and grind herself into him, anything to rid herself of the coiling tightness between her legs.

"No. I want to hear you," he groaned. "Give it to me, Lily. Show me what you like and how you like it. Let it go."

"Gabe…enough. I can't… It's too good."

"Too good, huh?" he breathed against her. "See. You're getting the hang of the ego-stroking thing, baby."

"It's too much. Please…"

He lifted his head. His dark eyes glittered, his lips glistened. The thought of what made them wet made it difficult for Lily to catch her breath.

"You really want me to stop, I will, but I want to make you come this way, with nothing but my mouth, my tongue. I know you're close, Lily."

God, it shouldn't be possible, should it? She'd already… And then she couldn't think because he'd put his mouth on her again, his wicked, relentless tongue lashing against her, into her, without mercy. She arched off the bed as she went over, the low moan ragged, her lower body jerking against him. He held her hips steady and stroked her through the pleasure with soft, mind-destroying licks.

When she could finally breathe, when she finally opened eyes that had been clenched tightly closed, his gaze was locked on her face.

"You're so fucking beautiful when you come. Those soft sounds you make… It's how I always know you're close. They drive me wild, every time."

Lily's heartbeat was just starting to slow when Gabe sat up and grabbed for one of the small packets. His entire body was rigid, tension in every line of muscle defined on his large frame, a light sheen of moisture covered his body. Oh God, he'd brought her to orgasm, twice, before thinking of himself. She watched, mesmerized as he tossed the packet aside and rolled the condom down his thick length in a casual one-handed move that had "expert" written all over it.

By the time he stretched his body over hers, pushing her back into the mattress, she could barely think for the thundering in her ears and the hard, insistent flesh between her legs.

"Comfortable?" he asked roughly as he eased her legs farther apart to make room for himself.

She swallowed. "Yes."

"Sure?"

She could only nod when he skimmed a hand down between their bodies to guide himself. She jumped as his fingers brushed against her sensitive flesh.

"Be sure because once I get inside you I doubt I'll care after that."

She didn't believe it for a second. "Gabe…"

He pushed forward slowly. It could have been only an inch, but he pulled almost all the way out and then back in ever so shallowly. He did it again and again. Her body screamed for him, needed the plunge of his heavy body and he was going to tease her?

"*Gabe.*"

He leaned down and closed his mouth over her breast, drawing the nipple into the hot wetness and flicking it with his agile tongue in the same maddening rhythm as his body into hers.

Lily arched off the bed at the sensation, jerking her hips against him in a futile effort to end the burning tension between her legs.

"Gabe, please I—"

He growled and plunged into her, all at once, sinking into her as far as he could go. His body shuddered and she grasped his shoulders for leverage as his hips began to slam against her, his thick cock spearing back and forth through flesh already swollen and sensitive.

A breath was forced out of her body with each of his thrusts and then she couldn't breathe at all. Pleasure burst through her, vibrating, radiating throughout her entire body with an intensity that should have shocked her, terrified her, yet all she could do was squeeze her eyes shut, hang on and ride through the sensations she'd only ever felt with him.

* * * * *

Lily stretched sometime later when he returned from the bathroom making no effort to hide her approval. He was unashamedly naked, not a modest bone in his entire body and why would there be? God, he was male perfection.

"I think you've corrupted me," she murmured as he sat on the side of the bed, his muscled back to her.

He turned his head to look at her. His eyes were red as if he'd rubbed at them, lines of fatigue were heavy around his mouth, his cheeks hollowed. She'd expected him to laugh, at least smile, but he just looked at her with that solemn way he had and everything inside her went still.

"Yeah, I probably am."

"Gabe—"

"I'm messed up, Lily. I'm not the same as I was…before."

Lily slowly sat up. "Well, I didn't know you before, so—"

"I can't be like I was. The things I've seen and heard… God the stuff I've done. If you act like a scumbag for long enough, talk like them, live like them, *fuck* like them…it rubs off."

"No."

A harsh laugh shot out of him.

She wrapped her arms around her drawn-up legs. "I know you're a good person, Gabe."

He laughed again and there was nothing pleasant about the sound. He got up, grabbed his clothes where he'd thrown them and began jerking them on quickly, roughly.

"You don't know shit about me. You invited me in here after knowing me, what, mere minutes? Christ, I could have been anyone. I could have—" He looked at her once he was dressed, his shirt still mostly unbuttoned. "How did you know— How were you so sure I wouldn't hurt you?"

She met his eyes, her gaze steady. "I knew."

"*How?*"

"I just did."

"Why? Because I was your fucking knight in shining armor that night?"

She drew in a shaky breath and frowned. "Instinct, I guess. I knew, deep down you were—"

"Yeah? You think you're an expert on me after a couple of rolls in the sack? You fuck a tow truck driver less than an hour after he picks you up and your fiancé had been screwing around behind your back for God knows how long. Not exactly stellar references, if you know what I mean. Forgive me," he drawled, "if I happen to question your judgment of character."

Lily swallowed against the lump in her throat and the cold numbness that radiated from her chest and down each limb. He... *God, he was right.* What the hell did she know anymore? All she could say for sure was that she'd been drawn to Gabe the instant she'd heard his voice and she couldn't really say why. Maybe she did have poor judgment, but it was probably more likely she should go with her gut more. She'd known, deep down, Ian was wrong for her. Just as she'd known she couldn't let Gabe walk away from her last night. Little good it did her now.

"Lily, look I..." Gabe took a deep breath. "Last night, sex with you...the beautiful sex with you...it's the first time I've felt clean in two years, clean enough to be in the same room as my family today, to be able to hug my mother. God, you smell like sunshine and fresh laundry, do you know that? I know I should have stayed the hell away from you—I knew it—yet I came back here anyway. Zach was right."

"Gabe—"

"You are more his type. You're more anyone's type than mine. I'm fucking toxic. You said it yourself. I'm corrupting you and I don't— I can still feel my skin crawling with it and I don't want the filth I've had to live with for the last two years to touch you in any way."

"Oh, Gabe..."

He stopped at the doorway to her bedroom and glanced back at her. His eyes looked black in the dim light. She ached to do something, anything to make it better, but the reality that he was going to walk was all she could grasp.

"I would have written you off as a classy, rich chick, completely out of my league, except..."

"Except?"

"Yeah, the freckles."

"Freckles?"

"Yeah, you have this little trail of freckles across the top of your nose. That and the way you ate me with your eyes."

As if she needed that reminder right now.

She cleared her throat, but it did little good. Her voice still came out uneven and hoarse. "May I give *you* some advice?" Lily managed, feeling the composure she'd somehow held onto fracture right along with her voice. "You're going to have a tantrum and walk out on a woman? You should probably do that *before* you fuck her."

Chapter Six

"Um…hello?"

"Can I come over?"

"Gabe?" Lily sat up, heart jumping, the fog of deep sleep gone in an instant at the familiar, rough voice in her ear. She glanced over at the clock on her nightstand.

"God, it's 3:30. In the morning."

"I know. I'm sorry. The sofa, I'll crash on the sofa. You won't even know I'm there."

"Are you okay?"

"Yeah, I'm…I just…*please*."

She hadn't heard from him in a week. Who did he think he was? Did he really expect he could just waltz back in here and pick up where they'd left off—wherever the hell that was? After the way they'd left things? The way *he* had? She wanted to tell him to go to hell, yet the edge of desperation in his voice tore at her. That and the plea he didn't seem to be able to stop. It probably made her an idiot, but she couldn't ignore it.

She sighed. "All right, but—"

Lily broke off as the line went dead and the doorbell rang. Heart jumping, she rushed downstairs, barely remembering to check the peephole.

It wasn't necessary.

"Oh my God, Gabe."

Despite that his bruising had completely healed, he looked awful. He stood with his hands thrust into the pockets of dark jeans, shoulders hunched against the crisp, cool air. His hair looked as if he'd gotten up and just ran rough hands through it and the t-shirt looked as if he might have slept in it. He didn't even have a jacket. Even in the dim light she could see the sharp lines around his mouth, the grooves in his cheeks and his darkly shadowed jaw.

"I'm fine. It's fine." His voice was ragged and raw. "I just need..."

"Are you sure you're okay?"

"Getting there. Now."

"And if I'd said no?"

He shrugged and raised his eyes to hers with a focus that was sharp and intense, in direct contrast to his ragged appearance. He took in her short, thin nightgown in a quick, searing glance that had her swallowing against the heat in his eyes.

"You have every right to tell me to go fuck myself. In fact, you probably should. I expected you to. Maybe I even wanted you to."

She reached out to draw him in, yet he stepped back out of her reach.

"Sorry. Not yet, okay?"

Lily frowned. He was edgy, his dark eyes shadowed. He looked even leaner, as if he hadn't been eating properly and tension swirled around him as if it were a living thing. Despite all the resolutions she'd made, despite all the self-assurances that things had worked out for the best, seeing him again only showed her that her body still yearned for him with a hunger she never would have thought possible, even as her mind told her it was foolish.

She stepped back as he eased past her, careful not to touch her.

"It's late. Come upstairs," she whispered.

Lily went to her room, conscious of Gabe following her, even though he didn't make a single sound. She stopped by the side of her bed, her hands going to the hem of her nightgown.

"I didn't come here for this. For sex," he ground out, his voice ragged, his gaze glued to the grip she had on her nightgown.

It was impossible to miss the massive erection straining the front of his black jeans. Her hand fell away.

"No? Then why?"

He was silent for so long, she didn't think he was going to answer.

"Lily..." He rubbed a hand roughly across his face. The rasp of his whiskers was loud in the heavy silence of the room. "I know I'm probably weirding you out, but...that night we spent together? It's the only night in over two years I've been able to sleep more than an hour at a time. I just wanted to... I thought...fuck, I don't know what I was thinking exactly, but I'm just so damn tired. I'm sick of being so damn tired."

Lily took off her nightgown in a single move and removed her panties. She got into bed, lay down and held the covers open for him. All she knew was that he was hurting, really hurting and she'd do something about it if she could. She couldn't do anything else.

He swallowed, his dark eyes tracing slowly over the slice of her body he could see. His jaw clenched, he closed his eyes and took a deep, unsteady breath.

"As much as I want to, I really didn't come here for this. I don't even have any rubbers with me. I didn't bring any because I didn't want you to think—"

"That's okay. I went out and got some."

His lids lifted and she shivered as he stared at her.

"They're in the bedside table," she added quietly.

Gabe pulled his gaze from her for a moment, leaned down to open the drawer and choked back a laugh. "Lily, there have to be ten boxes here."

Well, what did she know about condoms?

"I wasn't certain, there were so many different types, plus I wasn't sure what you'd prefer."

God, had that sounded totally pathetic?

His eyes closed briefly. "You bought them for us?"

She cleared her throat. "I was pretty sure I'd never see you again, but I..."

Lily forgot what she was about to say when he muttered something she couldn't catch, grabbed his shirt at the back of his neck and peeled the snug-fitting black t-shirt off in a single move. She licked her lips as he made short work of his jeans, pushing them down and off and kicking his shoes aside.

The angles and planes of his naked body, so different from hers, were starkly male. Every muscle was clearly defined on his lean body. They glided under his skin with every move he made. His erection stood out from his body, long and thick, his balls heavy beneath. God, he was so beautiful and her body reacted instantly. Heat flared low in her abdomen and she was wet, very wet, and burned for him.

Still he hesitated. "Lily, really, I didn't—"

"Shut up and get in here already."

Yeah, she'd tried to convince herself she'd never hear from him again, yet her mind, her *heart* had refused to accept it. She knew he'd probably be gone in the morning, maybe sooner, but right now her body cried out for him, wanted him, needed him.

"I'm not up for any fancy foreplay," he warned, still standing by the side of the bed, almost as if he was expecting her to change or mind. "I don't have the control right now for it. I just want to be inside you."

Her mouth went dry. "Me too. I mean, neither am I."

Her heart pounded as he bent to get into the bed. Already she could imagine the heated slide of his skin against hers, the weight of his body on her, the feel of his—

She jumped when his phone rang.

"Fuck." He yanked the phone out of a pocket in his jeans, looked at the screen and cursed again. "If I don't answer it, it'll never stop." He punched a button. "What?" he barked as he turned his back to her.

Lily swallowed at the sight of his broad, muscular back and smooth, lean buttocks. God, the back view was just as impressive. He had an incredible ass.

He sighed and ran his hand through his hair. "Yeah. Jesus, Zack."

Lily couldn't take his eyes off him as he moved restlessly back and forth, mesmerized by the slide of the muscles under his smooth skin with each movement.

"I'm fine." His eyes swung to her. "I'm with Lily." His eyebrows slashed down over his eyes. "None of your fucking business."

He hung up and flung his phone back on top of his jeans.

"Gabe—"

"I don't want to talk. Not now. I just want inside you. So bad."

He sheathed himself in record time, climbed under the covers and pulled her firmly against him. His skin was cold, a little clammy. She vowed she'd warm him, but he had her on her back and was braced over her in an instant. She shivered as his powerful thighs pushed hers apart and he put a hand down between them to guide himself.

Lily could feel how wet she was when he moved his cock up and down her slit, spreading her moisture, coating himself, and couldn't prevent the whimper that erupted from her. She forced her body to relax, knowing the treat that was in store for it.

She grasped the back of his shoulders when he pushed in, rocking back and forth, burying himself inside her—inch by slow inch—until he was lodged deep.

He swallowed. "Okay?"

He always asked when he entered her. She may never use "gentle" to describe him but he was always so conscious of her, so mindful of his strength and it undid her every single time.

"When you're inside me?" she managed. "I'm always more than okay."

"I'm sorry," he sighed.

"For?"

"The no foreplay thing. You must think—"

"I'm not exactly thinking right now, except maybe how good you feel."

He filled her, completely dominating her, his weight holding her immobile against the mattress. She tried to fling the covers off. When she couldn't manage it with her arms with the way he was holding her down, she tried to use her feet.

He frowned. "What are you doing?"

"I want to see you. I want to see your beautiful body, I want to feel and watch your muscles flex as you thrust into me."

Lily smiled when she saw the spots of color on his lean cheeks. He flung the covers back off the bed with a single, powerful flick from his wrist.

She sighed and skimmed her hands up and down his broad, powerful back, as far down as she could reach and across the slopes of his smooth buttocks. So hard. He was so hard all over. She closed her eyes as she felt his muscles begin to flex and roll under her hands, mirroring the sharp sensations of pure pleasure between her legs as he began to drive his cock in and out of her in a series of long, deep thrusts that had her to the brink almost instantly.

"Say my name," he grunted.

"Gabe."

"Again."

"God, Gabe."

"Yeah…"

He moved faster and faster, his balls slapping against the sensitive flesh between her legs as he moved his powerful thighs farther apart, opening her to him, to his thrusts.

"Oh, Gabe…"

"The looking and the watching?" he ground out between thrusts. "Goes both ways, babe."

Lily gasped as he rolled and she found herself on top of him, draped over his chest, her hands beside his head as he continued to drive into her from beneath, his hands caging her hips.

"Sit up," he growled.

Lily flattened her hands against his hard chest and levered herself upward somehow. She tried to keep her eyes open, but the pleasure was too intense, too sharp. She tilted her head back at the sensation as he kneaded her breasts with firm fingers, his rough palms grazing her nipples with each movement, in sync to the driving force of his body in hers.

"I get the feeling you like this position," she panted.

"I like *you* in this position," he forced out through clenched teeth.

She rolled her lower body forward and back, flexing her hips as she did so, contracting her internal muscles each time her body sank back down on his.

He groaned. "I did *not* teach you that."

Lily looked down at him with an effort, breathless at the sight of him beneath her, so big, so hard, so male. And so turned-on. By her. Arousal was etched into every angle of his face.

"Maybe you inspire me," she managed.

She reached out a hand to smooth the line between his brows and gasped when he deflected it with a sharp move and twisted her arm up behind her back.

He'd stopped moving inside her. His eyes were dark, tortured as he released his hold slowly.

"Sorry. Reflex."

Despite the quick, violent move he hadn't hurt her. She leaned down and placed her palm flat against his rough cheek, slowly, so he knew her intention.

"God, Gabe. What's been done to you?"

He closed his eyes briefly and she felt the tremor that went through him. His hands clenched on her hips. "I need to be in control now. I need to have you under me. I need *you*."

He flipped her beneath him with a move so fast she wouldn't have thought it possible and began thrusting with long, deep moves, his thrusts becoming faster and more forceful as he pounded into her. He spread his thighs, forcing her legs up and wide to accommodate him. He fit his elbows into the V of her knees, holding her open to him and completely at his mercy as he moved against her.

She gasped as his body slapped against hers and he went deep, deeper than he'd been before.

Once.

"Too hard?"

Twice.

"Lily?"

A third time. She groaned and arched a body that felt as if it didn't belong to her anymore.

"Lily? Is it too hard?"

"No, no, it's… God, Gabe. Faster, just a little faster."

Lily felt her eyes roll back in her head at the intensity of sensation, a blinding force of hunger and need quickly raging through her. All her nerve endings sprang to life, fed by the surging sensations between her legs. The force of it would have terrified her if she hadn't known him, hadn't known deep down and with everything in her that he would never hurt her.

She gave herself over to him completely, giving everything and anything of herself that she could. She barely heard her own gasps and cries over the deep growls against her throat as he slammed his body against her feverishly.

"Lily, Lily..."

His slick body jerked against her. A deep rumble erupted from him and then he was groaning and flexing against her with the power of his release. And knowing she'd given him that, had helped him achieve that degree of pleasure, it sent her careening over. And then there was nothing save for the most painfully sweet, searing pleasure she'd ever known and a deep-seated satisfaction that she'd been able to give him what he needed.

* * * * *

"How much foam would you like?"

God, how he'd missed this stuff. Mundane details, important for a second, intimate everyday things he hadn't had the luxury to be a part of for so long. He smiled. Not that anyone had ever asked him that particular question before.

"I'm going to go with...not much."

He leaned back against the cabinet and just watched her. She had a fancy coffee machine that looked as if it did everything except drink the coffee for you and she worked it like an expert. He was just enjoying the way she moved—that and the fact she looked hot as hell wearing nothing but his t-shirt. He kept getting these flashes from last night, how she'd sounded, how she'd felt when he'd been buried deep inside her, how she'd looked completely and utterly exhausted from their sex. And satisfied. Oh yeah, that look of satisfaction on her face would feed his fantasies for a long time to come.

He flexed his shoulders. He had marks. A lot of them. Scratches and gouges from her nails and he couldn't have been more pleased to bear the evidence of how far she'd been gone, how much pleasure he'd given her.

"You could totally work in one of those coffee shops doing that." He looked around and one shoulder lifted. "Not that you'd want to or that you need to."

"Gabe—"

"It's okay. It's obvious you're loaded."

Lily turned to him. "Not me. My family. They—"

"Yeah, I know all about your family."

She frowned. "You do?"

He looked her right in the eyes. It was ingrained in him, to know everything about his surroundings, who he dealt with, yet he'd had more than a driving need to know about her, everything and anything he could dig up. And he couldn't apologize for that, even if she took issue with it.

"I'm good at what I do, Lily. I know your father's some big-time defense attorney—high profile cases, mega bucks. Has his own firm. Your brother is all set to follow in his footsteps. Your sister is a renowned heart surgeon, your mother a regular on the charity circuit. I know your grandmother built and ran a food manufacturing empire by the time she, ah…died."

God, he saw the tightening of her lips and wanted to kick himself for just blurting it out. He'd dug up a lot more but he'd also discovered that she and the old woman had been incredibly close.

"This house, she left it to me in her will along with the means to take care of it." She fingered one of the diamond earrings she wore and he knew they hadn't come from a rich boyfriend. "She meant well. She just wanted me to be completely independent from them. My family, that is. They're all so very impressive and I'm…not. But I'm just not the same as they are—ambitious, overachievers. She understood that.

"They can be overbearing when they want something and she thought... Well, I've learned to stand up to them now, but they're still not at all happy I'm teaching at a public school. They think it's 'an incredible underutilization of the education I received'." She smiled. "She knew how much I always loved it here and that I'd never be able to afford it on my own. She left everything else to charity. They were all furious."

Yeah, he knew all that as well. And her family had been more than furious. They'd tried for years to have that part of the will overturned.

"I blew my cover," he forced out. "Two years and I blew it. Just like that."

She looked up in surprise at the outburst, but it was time he got it out. All of it.

"Oh, Gabe."

"I used to think there was good and bad, no middle ground," he said quietly. "It was why I became a cop. Now I know there are shades of both and bad so evil, most people couldn't even comprehend it. I was so fucking naïve."

"Was it worth it?"

"I ask myself that every minute of every day." He sighed. "It was about to go down. Everything we'd been working toward, waiting for. It was all set up. We were going to have them, all of them. A few of them...they wanted to celebrate. They showed up with a girl."

Gabe closed his eyes against the images, but it didn't do a fucking thing. It was burned into his memory. "It wouldn't have been the first time, but it was women who knew the score, knew what they were getting themselves into. Some of them really got off on it. This girl— God, they'd snatched her right off the street. By the time they got there, they'd already had her a couple hours. I..." He swallowed against the lump in his throat. "They'd risked everything with that dumbass move, drunk with confidence, but I couldn't reason with them. They were too high on adrenaline, on the deal that was about to make them a fortune. Not even knowing it was all about to come together, not even knowing the time, the effort, the fucking cost of what I'd been working toward. None of it mattered. I-I lost it. Blew my cover and everything went to shit."

"So, you saved her."

She'd already been traumatized, but he'd also been sure that girl wasn't going to be walking out of there alive. He'd seen the resolution in their eyes. And the madness.

"I put the entire mission at risk. I could have waited another Goddamn hour. Maybe—"

"But you saved her."

"Yeah," he sighed.

"And? After all that, did you have enough evidence to arrest them?"

He took a deep breath. He'd been so fucking lucky. The gunfire had mobilized the team already in place and they'd saved his ass. It could have easily all been for nothing. He could have easily been killed, the girl could have been killed in the crossfire, the whole setup could have fallen apart. His heart slammed against his chest. He could still smell that day as if it had just happened. "Yeah, we had enough on those of them left alive."

She put a hand on his arm. The touch was soft and light, but he felt it all the way down to the soles of his feet.

"I don't know all the details. I'm not qualified and I know my opinion doesn't count for much, but I know you would have done the only thing you thought you could at the time, what you thought was right."

He'd heard it all before, of course. "You're wrong."

She swallowed.

"It does matter what you think, Lily."

"That night you came to get me. Risking your own life for a woman you didn't know, hadn't met, had never even seen?

It wouldn't have mattered who it was. You would have gone in there anyway, wouldn't you?"

He shrugged. "Maybe I'm just an adrenaline junkie. I've lived on the edge of fear and discovery for so long, maybe I seek out danger, risk. Maybe that's the only way I can feel alive now."

It's what he'd agonized over for the better part of the last year.

She took a deep breath. "Aren't there people you could talk to? You know—"

"Yeah. And I did, it was required, but I just didn't think I needed it or that it would do anything."

"Maybe you should reconsider."

"I don't know." He paused. "Maybe." His dark gaze swung to hers. "Lily, it's still hard being back in my own skin. I don't exactly feel…stable yet."

Well, all except when he was with her.

"It's as if I've been living in a parallel universe for the last two years. I'm getting there, but it's going to take me some time before I can— Before I'll feel as if I'm part of *this* world again." He sighed. "In the meantime, I know I happen to be a moody, unpredictable jerk. And I'm really sorry for that."

He turned to the door. He knew what he was going to do, what he needed to do and he had to get the hell out of here.

She slipped in between him and the door, her back pressed up against it, blocking his path.

"Not this time," she said crossing her arms.

"Lily—"

"Dammit, Gabe, you don't get to just walk this time."

"Lily."

"Because I'm—"

"I'm not going anywhere."

He smiled at the rant she'd been ready to let fly, at the sparkle in her eyes, the frown between her brows and the color high on her cheeks. It all looked great on her. Yeah, she might look cool and elegant but it was all on the surface.

"I could list off ten reasons why it's dumb that I'm here, why I'm bad news for you, why I don't deserve anything you've given me, but last night? Yeah, that pretty much cured me of any thought I could walk away from you. So, I'm not going anywhere. Well, I am, I have some stuff to do, but I'll be back. I have some things—there's some stuff you should probably know. And after that? Well, you might just be glad to be rid of me."

* * * * *

"Gabe," Lily breathed when she opened the door a couple of hours later and saw what he held out in front of him.

Wow.

"They're...beautiful."

"It took me awhile to find them. They, ah, they're lilies, you know."

It wasn't the first time she'd been given lilies. In fact, Ian had really made a thing of it, but coming from Gabe it was just, well she wasn't sure exactly what except...unexpected.

Social etiquette and what to say in every situation had been drilled into her from the time she could talk. She'd had a lot of time to think about what he'd told her, but in this—with him—she had no idea what to say to make any of it better.

"Um, I guess I'll put them in water."

She walked to the kitchen, conscious of Gabe following. He watched her in silence as she hunted down a glass vase, filled it with water and set the flowers on the counter.

He took a deep breath as he stepped in close. "About your... That guy, that first morning."

Lily frowned. "Ian, he—"

Gabe put his hand over her mouth, his eyes hot on hers. It wasn't exactly a finger laid lightly across her lips. Oh no, he'd cupped his entire palm over her mouth, sealing her words in.

"I don't want any details," he rasped. "I don't think I could... I just want to know it's done. Over."

She nodded. It was pretty much all she could do.

He took away his hand. "Sorry. My imagination's been a bitch. I don't need any shred of reality to set it off. Okay?"

Lily licked her lips. "You sound almost..."

"Jealous? Yeah, and there's no 'almost' about it."

Lily's stomach jolted at that, especially when he pulled out a small, oblong, gift-wrapped package from his jacket.

"I got you something. I'd planned to get you a big-ass box filled with every style and color I could find, but... Well, I saw these and thought... Anyway, here."

He thrust it at her as if it suddenly burned his hand.

"Open it," he prompted gruffly when she just stared at it, at him.

Lily hadn't been sure what to expect. It certainly wasn't the skimpy white bikini-style panties she lifted from the box. They were her size. They were from her favorite lingerie store. And they had the words "I Love You" printed all over them in bold, black font.

She raised her eyes to his. His gaze was laser focused on her. The one that said she had his full and undivided attention, whether she wanted it or not. Her mouth went dry.

"I've never actually told a woman I loved her before and I never thought it would be with panties, but...dumb, huh?"

Oh God, breathe.

"They had a matching bra, but you said... I... *Christ*." He thrust a hand through his hair. "I'm really not very good at this stuff."

She tried to swallow, she did, but couldn't get her throat to work. "What stuff?" she managed.

"This...relationship stuff."

Breathe. In and out.

"Relationship?"

"You thought I wanted to just swing by here whenever I needed to get laid?"

Well...yeah.

He cringed at her look.

"I do want to— Get laid, that is, I'm a guy after all but it's not that I'm here just because of that. It's you, Lily, I'm here because it's *you*." He let out a rough breath. "God, I'm not making much sense here."

"Gabe, I'm not really sure..."

"See? I told you I'm fucking hopeless at this." He ran both hands through his thick hair. "All I know is I get hard just thinking about you and I think about you all the time. You know what that means? It means I have a permanent hard-on that no amount of jerking off gets rid of. The night you called me? I'd never met you, had never seen you, yet... God, you could have been sixty, you might have been married with a bunch of kids, yet your voice got me hard. I've never felt the way I do when I'm with you, when you're touching me, when you come for me. And coming doesn't make it go away, it just makes it...more. I feel it *here*." He slapped a hand to his chest, over his heart. "When I look at you. And when we kiss?"

He closed his eyes briefly and then his gaze blazed at her. "It's always just been another part of women and sex for me, a step in the process, you know, something women wanted, expected, yet with you..." His voice dropped. "I've never kissed you, not mouth-to-mouth while I've been inside you, have you noticed? I think I'd totally overload."

Lily felt the shiver course through her when he stepped into her and framed her face in his hands, tilting her head up to him. Heat blazed in response, throughout her body, low, between her legs.

"I should have been able to walk away from you that first night, you know? I told myself a decent guy would have, that I'd changed somehow...but it was just you. As soon as I touched you, I knew. You do it for me, Lily, like no other woman ever has."

Oh God, this man—gorgeous, strong, hot—had feelings? For her?

"I felt it that first night too," she whispered. "It's why I... I mean, I'd never done anything like that before, just inviting someone in that way."

"Yeah, I know. *Now.* I thought you were playing me, with the awkward, wide-eyed innocent act. I've become so used to figuring out someone's game, their angle, it took me awhile to realize you didn't have one."

"Gabe, I—you—we don't really know any—"

"Yeah, you do, all the important stuff anyway." He took a deep breath. "Gabriel Jackson. Thirty-two. Aries. Only child. Big, nosy extended family. Cop."

Oh God, until this very second she hadn't even known his last name.

"And I'm not going to be able to stop being a cop. I thought that I'd given more than should be expected of me, that I was done, but everyone was right. I was deluding myself about that. Every part of me, every cell in me has 'cop' written all over it."

"Gabe, it's—"

"I won't be doing undercover work again. My cover was blown wide open anyway."

"Gabe," she tried again.

"Being with a cop isn't easy and I'm not an easy kind of guy to begin with. I've been called intense. Oh yeah, for the record? I'm the faithful type. I'm not made any other way."

Oh God. The way he was looking at her.

"So, what do you think?"

Lily took a deep breath. "Ah…"

"I've probably been giving mixed signals."

She gave a weak smile. "You think?"

"I'm used to relying only on myself, I'm not used to needing anyone, but *dammit,* Lily I need *you* and I've never said that to another person before either. Ever."

Oh God. She could fall for this guy, really fall for him. That is, if she wasn't already there. She felt it, knew it deep inside. Not the so-so, compartmentalized, conventional feelings she'd had for Ian, but the heart-totally-and-completely-on-the-line kind of feelings. Love.

"So, you want to put me out of my misery here?"

Lily cleared her throat. "I just have one question."

His body tensed against her. "Okay."

She licked her lips and looked down at the panties still clutched in her hand. "Just the one pair?"

He frowned.

"I mean, these won't last long because I'll probably want to wear them everyday."

Just like that she felt some of the tension ease from him. "There's a hell of a lot of panties in that drawer upstairs I still want to see you in."

She smiled and he ran a thumb along her bottom lip. "I want to sleep next to you every night, skin-to-skin. I want the right to make love to you and I want it to be my obligation and mine alone to keep you safe—and satisfied. I want you to be my woman, Lily…exclusive, you know? No other guys." His hands settled on the curve of her hips, bringing her against him. His hardness was a brand against her. "Well, except for my fictitious brother on occasion. We'll let him watch, okay?" His voice lowered. "We've been talking. There's some other things we want to try."

The heat flared instantly between her legs, her thighs trembled, the flesh between her legs clenched. She swallowed. "There are?"

He laughed. "Yeah. You're gonna love it."

And then he sobered as he looked directly into her eyes, into *her*. "In case there's any doubt? I'd never share you with anyone, brother or not."

She shivered at the raw possessiveness, the heat in his gaze as he looked at her that said "mine", that said he'd do anything to take care of her, to keep her safe.

This is what she'd been missing, what she'd always craved but hadn't known it—to be wanted like this, to be needed, to know beyond a shadow of a doubt this man would go to any lengths, would sacrifice whatever he needed to. *For her.* And for her to feel the same way.

"Gabe..."

I love you. She hadn't said the words. They still felt too fragile, but she could see it in his eyes that he knew. Soon. She'd give them to him soon.

Oh. Fuck. Yeah.

Gabe closed his eyes as Lily trailed hot, opened-mouth kisses along his jaw. He was buzzed, buzzed with the knowledge she wanted him, that he was going to do his best to make her his and yeah, that he was going to have her under him in a matter of minutes. He smiled. After she nibbled on him some more.

"I want you to show me sometime," Lily whispered against his ear. His hands clenched on her hips. He swore he felt the sensation of her hot, moist breath the entire length of his cock. God, how he wanted to see her lips stretched around him again. He'd dreamed it enough times since.

He took a shaky breath. "Show you?"

She skimmed her fingertips along his aching length and he gritted his teeth. He shouldn't have been able to feel it so keenly through the thick denim, but when she touched him that way, well…whatever the hell she wanted was fine with him.

"Show you what, baby?"

She licked at his earlobe and his knees almost gave out. "What you said about jerking off. I think…yeah, I'd like to see that."

Also by Kaily Hart

eBooks:

Pay Up

Picture This

Play Me

Point Blank

About the Author

Kaily Hart, a seemingly straight-laced mother of four, left corporate America and a high-powered, lucrative career to be a stay at home mom. That lasted about four weeks, during which time she realized she had a deeply repressed dream to write— and *romance* at that! Who knew? By day, Kaily plays conservative wife and soccer mom, but at night crafts hot and steamy tales of romance and love with gorgeous heroes who wouldn't dream of leaving the toilet seat up. *Ever.* She's smart and sassy, at least in her own mind, and is trying her best to bring the alpha male solidly back to contemporary romance, one hot story at a time. Kaily bought her first book from Ellora's Cave in 2003. Never in her wildest dreams did she think one day she'd join their ranks as an author or that she'd be writing erotic romance. But now that she is, it just feels so right.

The author welcomes comments from readers. You can find her website and email address on her author bio page at www.ellorascave.com.

Tell Us What You Think

We appreciate hearing reader opinions about our books. You can email us at Comments@ElllorasCave.com.

Why an electronic book?

We live in the Information Age—an exciting time in the history of human civilization, in which technology rules supreme and continues to progress in leaps and bounds every minute of every day. For a multitude of reasons, more and more avid literary fans are opting to purchase e-books instead of paper books. The question from those not yet initiated into the world of electronic reading is simply: *Why?*

1. ***Price.*** An electronic title at Ellora's Cave Publishing runs anywhere from 40% to 75% less than the cover price of the exact same title in paperback format. Why? Basic mathematics and cost. It is less expensive to publish an e-book (no paper and printing, no warehousing and shipping) than it is to publish a paperback, so the savings are passed along to the consumer.
2. ***Space.*** Running out of room in your house for your books? That is one worry you will never have with electronic books. For a low one-time cost, you can purchase a handheld device specifically designed for e-reading. Many e-readers have large, convenient screens for viewing. Better yet, hundreds of titles can be stored within your new library—on a single microchip. There are a variety of e-readers from different manufacturers. You can also read e-books on your PC or laptop computer. (Please note that Ellora's Cave does not endorse any specific brands.

You can check our website at www.ellorascave.com for information we make available to new consumers.)

3. ***Mobility.*** Because your new e-library consists of only a microchip within a small, easily transportable e-reader, your entire cache of books can be taken with you wherever you go.
4. ***Personal Viewing Preferences.*** Are the words you are currently reading too small? Too large? Too... ANNOYING? Paperback books cannot be modified according to personal preferences, but e-books can.
5. ***Instant Gratification.*** Is it the middle of the night and all the bookstores near you are closed? Are you tired of waiting days, sometimes weeks, for bookstores to ship the novels you bought? Ellora's Cave Publishing sells instantaneous downloads twenty-four hours a day, seven days a week, every day of the year. Our webstore is never closed. Our e-book delivery system is 100% automated, meaning your order is filled as soon as you pay for it.

Those are a few of the top reasons why electronic books are replacing paperbacks for many avid readers.

As always, Ellora's Cave welcomes your questions and comments. We invite you to email us at Comments@ellorascave.com or write to us directly at Ellora's Cave Publishing Inc., 1056 Home Avenue, Akron, OH 44310-3502.

11992777R10130

Made in the USA
Lexington, KY
16 November 2011